JOAN HETZLER

A COLD CASE IN JULY:
A DEREK FIELDING MYSTERY
by
Joan Hetzler

Copyright © 2023 by Joan Elizabeth Hetzler
Published by Gordian Books, an imprint of Winged Publications
www.joanhetzler.com

All rights reserved. No part of this publication may be reproduced, stored in a retrieval system, or transmitted in any form or by any means—for example, electronic, photocopy, recording—without the prior written permission of the copyright owner. The only exception is brief quotations in printed reviews.

This is a work of fiction. Names, characters, places, and incidents are either the product of the author's imagination or are used fictitiously, and any resemblance to actual persons, living or dead, business establishments, events, or locales is entirely coincidental. The publisher does not have any control over and does not assume any responsibility for third-party websites or their content.

ISBN-13: 978-1-959788-86-7

i

Chapter 1:
Cold Case in July

Derek listened to Megan's sweet but off-key voice singing in the shower as he dressed for his new job. Not her true talent, but as a newlywed he was still delighted to hear her voice in his house and in his life. He realized love may be blind but not necessarily deaf.

The singing stopped, the sound of the shower stopped, and the sound of the sliding glass door replaced both sounds. Soon Megan popped her head around the corner with a towel on her head and a terry cloth robe belted around her. Her short brown curls escaped the towel. "You look really nice in that suit. Are you off to teach the cold case team how to do their job?"

Derek glanced at her as he combed his hair. "There's not much of a team, just me. I'm off to offer a neutral trained mind after ten years on the Atlanta homicide squad to find any missed leads or clues. According to Sheriff Tagger, the victim was related to or worked with, not only all the suspects, but most of the politicians, judges, and police in the town."

Megan disappeared back into the dressing room and the sound of a hair dryer buzzed for several minutes. Then her voice came through slightly muffled. "How long has it been since the murder? And why haven't they solved it with all these new forensics methods?"

"It's been four years, and they have few clues. Tagger is tired of all the innuendos about his department and recently an ongoing political race between two of the candidates has resulted in new accusations on both sides. He thought I could look at the persons of interest and the victim with an unbiased and fresh approach."

"Ah, sounds perfect for you to do while waiting to start law school in a couple of months. But you forgot to add that he wants your brilliant mind that makes you such a successful detective." Megan stepped back into the room wearing her own business suit and curling her now dried hair.

Derek grinned and stepped over to kiss her nose. "I thought that was too obvious to mention."

Megan grinned and kissed him back. "Well, Sheriff Tagger must know it if he asked you to take on this project. Who was the victim again?"

Derek eyed Megan thoughtfully. She had her own way of finding and solving mysteries outside of her role as an investigative reporter for an international Christian ministry. "He was a county commissioner who was also a criminal attorney with his own firm. That's why he knew the judges and police and everyone else. He grew up there and many are related to him."

Megan leaned over to put on a light covering of makeup in front of the mirror. Another adjustment that came with marriage–sharing the mirror–not that he minded. Derek finished adjusting his tie and said, "He was shot in the head while sitting in his office chair behind his desk. The gun wasn't found, and the bullet did not match other shootings. The cleaning lady discovered him early on the morning of July 5th, but he had been dead about 8 hours. So, he was killed during the night of July 4th when the town was full of people listening to a fireworks concert and shooting their own firecrackers."

"So no one would notice gunshots. Was he married?"

"Yes, but his wife says they were separated. She had gone to stay with her sister who is married to the mayor."

"Did she say why they separated?"

"Just that she was tired of him wasting money and making snide comments about her family. Also, their youngest child just left for college, so she didn't need to 'put up with him anymore.' That's a direct quote from her I'm told."

Megan smiled. "A lesson for us to learn. Don't waste our money."

Derek laughed, "Since you gave up your high-powered journalism career to work for a nonprofit, and I've left my career for law school, I could ask 'what money?'"

Megan picked up her laptop computer case and car keys. "I guess, in that case we don't need to worry about 'wasting' it. If you want some help in solving this mystery, please let me know. I don't have any really demanding projects right now. Just some articles about how new laws are limiting church expansion in a Midwest state."

Derek also picked up his keys. "Thanks. It's really

a matter of reading the notes and evidence with fresh eyes. I might need to do some more interviews." He leaned over and kissed Megan before they both left for work. Each drove in a different direction.

As he drove along one of Atlanta's many four-lane roads leading out of the city, Derek's mind shifted to his new job. For 15 years he had worked as a police officer in the Atlanta metro area and the last 10 years as a homicide detective. His new role took him to a small town in rural north Georgia. The Sheriff had become of friend of his and asked him to look into the cold case. Derek rather looked forward to the challenge. He had never taken on a cold case before.

Until he met Megan most of his cases were fairly standard police procedure with no suspects trying to kill him. Megan had a way of investigating that left her a target or someone near her. But that shouldn't happen with a cold case. It would probably be mostly reading and analyzing the case notes, at least he hoped so.

Derek pulled into the Sheriff's office just off the town square in the city of Lahillsville, population 5,025, in the county of Stansboro. Local businesses, shops, and restaurants fronted the sidewalks around the main square. The entire downtown area consisted of about three blocks on all sides. The buildings lining the square were mainly of two-story red brick built in the late 19th century. Concrete benches circled a decorative fountain outlined in summer flowers. He would explore the town later. The victim's office and crime scene were in one of those red brick office fronts.

Walking into the police building, he smiled at the woman behind a glassed-in counter and introduced himself. She led him to Sheriff Tagger's office where a man in his early fifties with greying hair at the temples stood to shake hands. He looked like his desk job fought against his fitness regime and sometimes won.

Sheriff Tagger said, "Glad you can take this project on. How is Megan? Has she recovered from her encounter with the killers?"

"Yes, she's fine now and back at work."

"I guess congratulations are also in order to you on your recent marriage."

Derek grinned, "Yes, that too."

Tagger nodded. The small talk done and finished, he said, "When we first spoke a few weeks ago, this was a project I hoped you would take on. Now it has become more pressing. As our county commission race heats up, not only are two of the candidates accusing each other of the murder, but both are claiming my office covered it up."

Derek leaned against the back of his chair and crossed one leg over his knee. He looked thoughtful. "Were you the Sheriff then or an investigating officer?"

"I had been Sheriff for about two weeks and an officer for about ten years before that. The thing is, I knew Adam Cranford and didn't like him, and everyone knew it. It seemed every arrest I made, even of known career criminals, he managed to paint me as an abusive cop who had been mean to his delicate and misunderstood client. It didn't matter if that client beat up his wife so bad she was hospitalized or his client didn't know how that bag of cocaine got in his car's glove compartment."

Derek grinned. He had encountered similar situations with criminal defense attorneys who were outraged at his arrests made with irrefutable proof of guilt. "I know the type. It must have been hard in such a small town always having to deal with him."

"It was. Most of the time, the jury or the judge, depending on the case, could see the evidence for themselves. But there were a few criminals that got off that I still can't figure out how."

"Corruption?"

Tagger shrugged. "No proof and no way to know now. Sometimes in a very small town or very rural county, it's a question of an attorney calling up a friend and saying let's do such and such. I've seen both civil and criminal attorneys avoid court by making deals by word of mouth, to heck with ethics or the law."

Derek asked, "So what do you hope to achieve by hiring me? I can't guarantee I'll find the murderer or sufficient evidence if I did."

Tagger said, "I can say I hired an independent expert, an experienced homicide detective, to look at the evidence and the notes. That should stop some talk and accusations. If you find the killer, so much the better."

"How far can I go with this? Interviews? Ask for forensic tests if I see the need?"

"All of that. I plan to deputize you, so you can carry a weapon and make an arrest if you need to. Also, I have set up a temporary office for you down the hall with the paper case files and a computer to access our Department's programs. I don't want any of that material to leave this building, but I'm sure you know that. Otherwise, do what you need to. We've already agreed on your pay rate, but I know you have limited time so set a deadline of two months? How does that sound?"

"Sounds good. Before I get into the weeds, it would be nice to have a vision of the forest. A review of what you've done and the main persons of interest, if any."

Tagger tapped his fingers on his desk. "I'm not sure that's a good idea. I don't want to influence you one way or the other by my prejudices."

Derek looked at Tagger for a moment weighing the older man's words. "I see your point, but you know the people involved and have law enforcement instincts that cannot be gained by an outsider just reading the notes. Also, don't underestimate me. I've spent years sifting the wheat from the chaff of interviewee's statements."

Tagger nodded. He leaned back in his comfortable desk chair and narrowed his eyes at the ceiling as though he could see a movie unfurling of four years ago. "Very well. It was about this same time of year, long hot humid days just before the 4th of July. But things other than the weather were heating up...."

Chapter 2:
Stansboro County Four Years Earlier

"Just like now, it was an election year with several county commission seats up for re-election as well as other offices. Adam was the incumbent commissioner on the seat for his district that included our new industrial park. Several wealthy landowners as well as many residents of a nearby subdivision were very angry with him. They said that he was sneaking in a toxic and bad smelling chicken processing plant that should not be located so close to their homes. One of the landowners, Freda Faulkner, was also a real estate broker. She said the plant would reduce the value of her land and scare off future buyers. Freda also claimed Adam got a cut of bringing the business here and failed to put it up for a timely public discussion or a vote.

"The political fireworks started on Sunday, July 3rd, at a church homecoming picnic held on the grounds. Adam and his wife, Sharon, attended along with the entire church congregation. Freda showed up and stood at the end of the buffet line as people picked up their silverware. She was dressed in her Sunday best and said, 'Hi ya'll. Glad to see you. I just know God is unhappy over what Adam has done to our land here in the county. He's following in the way of that first Adam and ruining our beautiful garden by bringing in toxic businesses that don't mind fouling our air (no pun intended) and destroying our water. I'm running for county commission for this district, and I ask that you vote for me. You know I care about our county, and I would never sell my friends down the river for an illegal kickback. Please take one of my flyers and sign my petition to have Adam investigated.'

"Adam was a short chubby man in his mid-fifties who grew up in the county and knew everyone. He had been a football player and popular enough when younger. As the years passed he lost that popularity. His wife, Sharon, was tall and thin and aging gracefully. She had also grown up in the county and married Adam out of high school. His family was land poor whereas hers had both land and wealth. Most folks respected her as a charitable woman who helped a lot of folks in need. On this day, Adam set down his plate of fried chicken and green beans and walked over to where Freda stood. He was too smart to make a scene, but you could tell he was angry. He said, 'Why, Freda, are you doing more of that playacting of yours? More *'amateur' productions?* Or are you trying to find buyers for that termite infested Victorian mousetrap you want to sell north of town?'

"Freda replied, 'The truth will set you free, Adam. You have tricked and stolen from this county for the last time. Why didn't you put it up for a vote before inviting the owners in on that large plant to negotiate with the county? Why did you make it sound like they made chicken statutes instead of turning dead chickens into fertilizer?'

"'Careful, Freda, there are defamation laws. I can

sue you and that real estate business you don't understand. I'll put a lien on that house you inherited and sue Bob since its marital property. You better not accuse me of theft or fraud.'

"'Truth is a defense to defamation. I think a good court case with discovery will show us just how corrupt you are, just like your clients.'

"Sharon Cranford stepped beside her husband and said, 'Stop it you two. This is a church picnic. Freda, you can run for commissioner without trying to get Adam arrested.'

"'It's about time one of the criminals in this town was arrested and not set free by one of Adam's judge friends. Is that new Sheriff Tagger paid off too? Here, Sharon, why don't you sign the petition? You could help put this bag of wind in jail and get a good divorce settlement to marry William.'

"'What!' exclaimed Sharon. 'How dare you accuse me of seeing William?'

"'Not 'seeing' but certainly 'looking'. Don't you get tired of seeing your money go to stupid investments and schemes that fail? Remember your family had much more successful businesses twenty years ago, and Adam has ruined them with his poor business decisions. Our county needs a better commissioner, and you do too as a resident.'

"'I will not sign your petition.'

"Adam said, 'Go away Freda. Sharon's not that stupid. She knows I'm the one who makes the money in this family, and William is not the brightest bulb in the box. He just does what I tell him to do. He would never marry her, even if I divorced her.'

"Sharon turned on Adam, 'What do you mean I know

you're the one who makes money? I still own shares in the lumberyard, the Southern Style restaurant and the lease to the stores renting on Main Street."

"'That's just hanging on to what you got. I'm increasing our wealth.'

"Sharon hissed in her breath and exclaimed in a voice I had never heard her use.'Well, I'd like to know what account it's in. You aren't giving me any. How dare you say that about our finances?" Her face rigid and white from rage, she said, "Where is that petition, Freda?'

"Adam in his usual oozing way that was too friendly and reasonable had made Sharon angry for the first time anyone had ever seen. She signed the petition and went home and packed up and the next day moved in with her sister, Cece, who was married to the mayor of the town.

"Freda continued to walk around the church grounds handing out her flyers and getting people to sign the petition until a summer afternoon thunderstorm opened up and rain poured down. The sudden shower cooled off the air but not tempers.

"William Dunn, whom Freda accused Sharon of liking, was Adam's only law partner in the firm. He was a widower raising a young daughter after his wife died of cancer. He had a good reputation as an attorney and as an Elder in the church. When he heard of Adam's statements that afternoon, several witnesses said he started talking to Freda about buying a new office building to go out on his own.

"Whether he liked Sharon or not back then, is not known, but they have since married. William is running for Adam's old seat against Freda who won it after

Adam's murder. Hence, they are accusing each other of the murder. Supposedly William's motive was to marry Sharon, and Freda's motive was to get the commissioner's seat to put a stop to the new plant and help real estate values."

Derek listened to the tale of simmering passions unleashed in a small Georgia town. He said, "So, as far as motives that makes three known plus the residents not looking forward to smelling dead chickens instead of their gardens and trees."

"Three?"

"Freda, Sharon, and William."

"Ah, I guess I never considered Sharon seriously. She was, is, a throwback to the genteel lady who never raises her voice, is always kind and sweet, does good works and bakes for cake sales."

"Even nice ladies shoot their husbands."

"True, but I'm not sure she would have the skill."

"Wasn't it close up?"
"Yes, but not that close. It was about 50 feet and a single bullet right through the center of the forehead."

Derek raised his eyebrows. "I didn't realize that."

Tagger sighed. "Whoever did this was incredibly lucky or planned it very cleverly. Adam was sitting at his desk chair with his arms on the desk. Someone came in the unlocked front door into the reception area. His inner office door was open. That someone stepped just inside or outside his doorway, raised an arm and shot him. Then that person left. The timing was perfect because it was during the fireworks display with explosions, hundreds of people filling the square looking away from his door to the sky, and everyone carrying bags or something to hide a weapon in. The coroner estimates he died about 10:00 p.m. to 10:30 p.m., but that's not exact. For the record, the concert started at 9 p.m. and ended with the fireworks display at about 10:00 p.m. The display ended about 10:30 or 10:40 p.m."

"What about forensics?"

"Useless in this case. Half the town went in and out of their firm's offices as clients or to pick up legal forms or just to visit. The carpet had not been cleaned recently and showed countless tracks."

"So really the only clue is that he or she was a good shot?"

"Pretty much. Except there was one odd thing. When we removed the body, we discovered that Adam had a bunch of twenty-dollar bills clutched in his right hand. It totaled about $250.00. Looks like when he was shot, he grabbed at his chest with the money in his hand. Maybe he was going to put it away or maybe he was counting it, but nothing was stolen that we could see. Of course, we didn't know how much he had to begin with or why it was there. But still, it's odd the killer didn't take it."

"That is odd. Why was Adam sitting at his desk on a night of celebration and partying?"

"Good question. Could have been he had an appointment with someone, but if so, it wasn't on his calendar. Or, it could have been he was working late and catching up on planning how to defeat Freda. Or, maybe he was avoiding going home since Sharon took off that afternoon."

"What about the door? Wouldn't he have locked it with that many people milling around outside while counting his money?"

"You and I would have, but Adam never seemed to worry about threats from unhappy clients or ordinary break-ins. He had a way of avoiding conflict by convincing his enemies they imagined the whole thing."

"So, he did have clients found guilty?"

"Yes, and there are some who've made threats, but all were in jail."

"A paid hit?"

"Maybe, but how to find out and prove it?"

"What caliber bullet?"

"9mm. If we ever find the gun, we can try to match it. We did test all the handguns from the suspects, including Sharon who had one, but no match."

Derek nodded. "Did he handle divorce cases or other types of law? I've heard of more than one divorce attorney being shot and killed."

"Yes, so have I. He did a few for friends but none recently and none that were acrimonious."

"I see why you ran into a brick wall. Looking out further, what about the children? They are in their twenties. Any resentments or desire for a big inheritance?"

"Not that we could discover. Adam was not wealthy. He had sold most of his family's land and spent the money on get rich quick schemes. Sharon did have most of the money, but she handled it better than Adam. I think it was a sore point between them and why Sharon reacted so strongly at the picnic. Some people just don't have a head for business, and he seemed to get involved with schemes that lost money. For example, he invested in a 'dude ranch' that no one came to because it was poorly run and too close to town. His two children, a boy and a girl, each finished college and are now married. The son is the oldest and has two small children. Neither has shown any homicidal tendencies that I've seen."

"Did he owe anyone money?"

"Not a lot. We went through his accounts, but nothing jumped out at us. Sharon inherited everything because, ironically, he did not have a will."

"Attorneys can think they will live forever, also."

Tagger shook his head. "Adam was a piece of work. He never screamed or yelled at anyone. He was always the gentleman and smiled at you and paid you compliments while he cheated you out of money or defeated you in the courtroom. I'm not surprised he had enemies. The question is which one planned a murder? Or which one let anger get out of control on the one night they could get away with it?"

Derek could see his work was cut out for him. But he liked a challenge, and this seemed to be a fine one.

Chapter 3:
Sharon Olivia Martha Vincent Cranford Dunn

Sheriff Tagger led Derek to a temporary office and handed him a box of evidence as well as the password to the computer. After a quick explanation on how to use their software, the Sheriff left.

Derek took off his jacket and laid it over a nearby chair. He loosened his tie and began to read about the case notes. Then he looked at the persons of interest. His first choice was Sharon Olivia Martha Cranford who was now Sharon Olivia Martha Cranford Dunn. As the saying goes, "always investigate the spouse first."

Derek found it particularly interesting that Sharon objected to Adam's insults about her business skills but did not mention his slurs against William. He began to read. According to Sharon, she had been at her sister's house that evening. However, the sister, Cece, and the mayor, Andrew, could not confirm she stayed there all evening. They went to the 4th of July fireworks.

Curious to learn more about her, he signed up for a local library account to access their newspaper archives. He found many pictures of Sharon under her maiden name. She had been homecoming queen, president of the Lahillsville Women's Club three times, served on several church committees and also ran her father's sawmill and other inherited businesses. Few, if any, pictures showed her with Adam. Twenty-five years earlier, the two of them appeared as an engaged couple and then a photo of their wedding in the community section. Adam had pictures alone as the school's top quarterback and later when he had his law license and announced his practice. More recent photos showed him giving talks as a political candidate and on the county commission.

Derek looked up Sharon's address and decided to make a surprise visit. Almost certainly, an appointment would result in both her and her husband, as her attorney, present. He preferred to talk to her alone, at least at first.

Sharon still lived in the house she had inherited from her father that became hers and Adam's marital home and now hers and William's. Just a few miles north of town, he turned on to a paved road that ran between wide pastures and tall grass ready for cutting. Mountains stood in the distance covered with forest. He enjoyed the beautiful drive after his many years of fighting Atlanta traffic.

A surprisingly small house distinguished by its age rather than elegance appeared at the end of the trip. Flower beds surrounded ancient trees, and on one side, older but well-maintained stables showed a few horses grazing outside them. Just behind the house he could see a tall wire fence enclosing a backyard. The initial impression was of thrift and a love of family through the years.

Derek stepped on to the wide wooden porch with dark green Victorian carved railings and red petunias hanging in large planters. He knocked on the older wavy, paned glass.

Sharon came to the door and looked through it at him. She wore a simple cotton dress with a plain white collar and a belt tied at the waist. No jewelry. He held up his badge and identification. She cautiously opened the door a crack.

He said, "I'm Derek Fielding, the cold case detective that Sheriff Tagger hired to look into your husband's death. He said he had let the family know he was doing that."

"Yes, he did. I just, well, I didn't expect you to visit me, I mean today. I wish you had called." She opened the door wider and allowed him to step into the house.

He smiled slightly. "I'm sorry to interrupt you. I'm here temporarily and after going over the case files, I had a few questions for you."

Sharon frowned. "You know, young man, I've been married to two attorneys, and I'm not going to be questioned about a murder without one present. Let me call William and ask him to come out." She reached for an older landline phone sitting on a small table.

"Of course, I understand. I would like to speak to him also. I wanted to get a quick start as the Sheriff wants to put a stop to all these accusations against innocent people and find the killer."

Sharon's hand paused.

Derek continued, "Actually I didn't want to ask about the night of the shooting but to learn more about Adam. I'm trying to get a clear picture of him as a man and his personality."

Sharon pulled back her hand. "I'd rather not bother William if it's not necessary. If that's all you want to ask....." A burst of children's laughter came from the back of the house. "My daughter-in-law and grandchildren are here. Why don't we sit on the front porch? Let me tell them where I am."

Derek nodded and waited while she walked to the back. He didn't want to let her out of his sight and was prepared to follow. However, she stopped at the entrance to a door. When she opened it, he could see a swimming pool in the backyard with children laughing and swimming. She said, "Marilee, I have a guest and will meet with him on the porch. If you need anything let me know."

A young woman's voice sounded from somewhere, but he couldn't hear the words. He waited for Sharon to walk past him and lead him out to the porch where they both sat in chairs. It was not lost on him, a Southerner, that she had not offered him any refreshment, which was almost required of any hostess of a certain age in the South. That told him several things. She wanted him gone as soon as possible, and she didn't want to have this talk, at all.

She sat down in a wooden rocking chair, pushed back bangs damp from the hot humid weather, and said, "So what do you want to know about Adam?"

"I'm trying to figure out who the real Adam was."

Sharon frowned. "What do you mean?"

"I hear conflicting descriptions of him. On the one hand, he's a clever lawyer but a very poor businessman. I hear he's an aggressive attorney but avoids confrontations."

Sharon sat back and closed her eyes. In repose her face looked much younger, and he could see she had been very beautiful as a young girl. She was still attractive but in a more matronly way. "I guess that is conflicting. I hadn't thought about it."

"Was he always like that?"

"No, actually he was different when we were young. He was a daydreamer and wanted to travel and see the world."

"That seems a different personality than the man who was a star football quarterback."

Sharon smiled. "That was mostly strategy. He was very good at outthinking his opponents several plays ahead. He never tried to bully or overpower anyone. Everyone liked him back then, well except for Daddy. He didn't want me to marry him."

"Why was that?"

"I thought at first it was just that no boy was going to be good enough for his youngest daughter. But later I realized he didn't like Adam. He said he was no good. In fact, Daddy told me he had a long talk with Adam. He told him if he ever hurt me or cheated me out of my inheritance, he would have him to deal with and it wouldn't be pretty." Sharon sighed. "I wish Daddy was still around. He died about 15 years ago of a heart attack."

"I have to ask, did Adam ever hurt you or cheat you out of money or cheat with another woman?"

"He never physically hurt me but 'cheat' out of money? I don't know. I've wondered sometimes. He sure lost a lot of my money, but I thought that was his poor business sense. If he cheated with another woman, I never saw a sign or heard a whisper about it. At first, we were happy. Adam wanted to travel after he started working as a lawyer. We tried, but I got seasick on a boat. I just didn't like going to places where I couldn't understand the language or know what kind of food was on my plate. I got homesick, not just seasick. Then our first child came, and it was really hard to carry a baby or toddler, so we stopped."

"Did Adam travel by himself?"

"No, he seemed to give up that idea. Of course, most of the money was mine from my family's trust fund. Adam didn't make much as a young attorney. He couldn't just take off alone using my money, at least not without Daddy putting a stop to it."

"One thing does puzzle me. From the case notes, I can see where your husband insulted you about your business skills, but he also insulted both you and William. You defended your business skills but not the references to William never marrying you."

Sharon pushed back her bangs again. Derek was also feeling the humidity and midday heat in his jacket, but some conversations could not be rushed. She said, "Some things are best left unsaid. What should I have said? 'Oh yes, he'll marry me' or 'he's a kind and honorable man, but you're not.' How would that have helped the situation?"

"So, you just left?"

"Yes. Adam crossed an unspoken line that day. We couldn't pretend and put up a front anymore, and I didn't want to try. Also, to claim I was not able to manage money was ludicrous. He was the one who lost our money. I came home and prayed and cried. The next day, I packed a bag and went to my sister's house."

"You went there in the afternoon?"

"Yes. I stayed in the guest room and cried and read my Bible and prayed. I try to be a good Christian and didn't want a divorce. But I planned to ask for a financial accounting for a formal legal separation. After a while I took a sleeping pill because I could hear the explosions from the fireworks. Andrew and Cece went to it. The next day, Andrew told me that Adam had been shot. I couldn't believe it, I mean it was, but it seemed so odd."

"In what way 'odd'?"

Derek looked up as the front screen door popped open and a young woman stepped out. "I'm sorry to disturb you, Mama Dunn, and your guest, but I'm making a fresh batch of iced tea and wondered if you'd like a glass. Also, I just got the twins out of the pool, gave them a shower, and put them down for a nap. Will that mess up your plans if we stay a little longer?

Sharon raised her eyes and looked at the cheerful young woman. She smiled, "No, not at all, hon. I'm glad to have you here. You do what you want. I would like a glass of tea. Would you like some tea, uh, uh, officer."

"It's Detective Fielding, and I would love a glass." He looked up at the young woman and said, "Thank you for the offer."

She smiled and stepped inside.

Sharon looked ashamed. "I should have offered...well, never mind. You asked how it was odd. I think because Adam was so good at avoiding direct confrontations. He was very cagey and to be caught like that where he could be shot just didn't make sense."

"Can you explain a little more?"

"He...well.. he would always delay an explanation or diffuse an argument. He would say someone had misunderstood. He was caught by surprise, too, from what the Sheriff said. Adam always planned out his strategy."

Derek said, "Those traits would work well in business. How did he lose your money?"

Sharon paused to accept the cold sweat-beaded glasses with a slice of lemon on the rim from her daughter-in-law. She handed a glass filled with cold tea to Derek also.

She took a sip and said, "Not long after Daddy died, Adam talked me into investing in this Dude Ranch, but everything went wrong. The manager seemed to make people mad. Adam bought the wrong kind of horses, not gentle mares, but young high-strung horses. Our guests were learning to ride, and one or two were hurt and threatened to sue. Supplies were stolen. We had good reviews in the papers and some nice posts on social media, but it just seemed to be a money pit."

"Did you look at the books?"

"Oh, no, I wasn't involved in the management."

"But as an investor you had that right."

"It didn't occur to me. I mean I put the money in a joint account for him to use. There was no signed agreement that I was an investor. I didn't want to insult Adam. He could be very sneaky at times about getting someone back for something that made him mad. Also, I could see they had the wrong horses, and the manager was not very good. I was glad when it closed."

Derek didn't normally take refreshments from the suspects he interviewed but made an exception today. He was grateful for the cool drink. "Do you still have a copy of those books?"

Sharon also sipped her tea and frowned. "I don't know what happened to those accounts. They weren't in his personal papers when we did probate. I guess he threw them out after the required seven years the IRS says to hold documents."

Derek nodded. "Was that the only money he lost?"

"No, he lost some more of our money, mostly mine, when he bought some shares of a company a friend of his started. But the 'friend' ran off to the Cayman Islands and left everyone holding the bag. As I said, he had poor judgment on business ventures. And then at one point he said he had to declare bankruptcy due to money he owed for a restaurant he purchased that failed. I didn't want to lose my family's home, so I paid his bills."

"Yet, he seems to be successful as an attorney."

"Yes, that he could do."

"He must have made good money as an owner of his own firm."

Sharon looked out to the distant mountains and concentrated. "He always said he lived in a small town and couldn't charge the same big fees as Atlanta attorneys. Also, he said being a criminal attorney meant many of his clients weren't rich."

"Why didn't he branch out and do other law?"

"Sometimes he did. But he spent a lot of time on that county commission seat. I think he liked influencing people and knowing everything that's going on in the county. He made money, but we weren't rich. He did pay for both children's college tuition."

Derek finished his tea and set the glass on the porch side table. "Do you have any idea why he was in his office that night? Was that typical for him to work on a holiday like that?"

Sharon shook her head. "No idea. It was typical for him to work late at night but not on a holiday. That might be because I left, but we stopped going as a family years ago. He was more likely to go on his own and campaign for the upcoming election."

Derek nodded. He said in a gentle voice. "I know this has been difficult for you. I really want to thank you for helping me to understand Adam better. Hopefully, we can clear it up and remove a cloud of suspicion from those who don't deserve it."

Sharon looked relieved. "I do want to say that William and I...well nothing was going on four years ago. I did like him, and he liked me, but he had no motivation to shoot Adam."

Derek didn't want to point out that as a business partner to a devious and unethical man William might have a very good reason. Instead, he said, "I can see you take your Christian faith seriously, and I've heard William does also."

"Yes, that's just it. He's an Elder in the church and genuinely loves the Lord. From what I've learned since that night William was going to separate from the firm and start his own. He would never shoot Adam."

Derek stood up and smiled. "Thank you. I appreciate your help."

Sharon nodded, but the concern didn't quite leave her eyes as he turned to leave.

Chapter 4:
Tammy (Office Assistant)

Derek turned up the SUV air conditioning full blast and took off his jacket and tie. The noonday heat made both items of clothing unnecessary. Lunch had a nice sound, so he decided to try out the cafe on the square before further investigation. The small restaurant boasted several empty tables. He sat down at one close to the large window to write up a few notes while he ate and watched the local townsfolk.

Sharon had added more conflicting information to Adam's personality and abilities but cleared up a few minor points. His poor business decisions still conflicted with his clever legal skills, but she did explain why Adam became so careful and devious in his approach to people. Her father had a sharp eye on Adam and was protective of his daughter's money, health, and happiness. Adam apparently put his planning and strategy skills to use early on in getting what he wanted out of life.

A waitress came to hand him a menu, which offered mostly sandwiches and soup. A ham sandwich and tea suited him fine. He said, "I'm surprised I could find a table at noon. I'd think you'd be really busy located here on the square."

The waitress, a young girl, who looked like she had taken a summer job during high school said, "Yes, we're normally busy, except on Wednesday when the banks and lots of shops close at noon. But this weekend is 4th of July holiday and a lot of people have taken this week as a vacation since Friday's the official day off."

"I guess the 4th is pretty crowded then?"

"Oh, yes, at least at the concert and fireworks display. Lots of people bring their families and have picnics in a nearby park or here on the square which is closed to traffic."

"So, no one can drive up and park at the buildings here on the square that day?"

"No sir. People park in the grocery store parking lot or maybe all the way down at the recreation center and golf course, then they take the shuttle bus that runs back and forth."

"Mmmmm. What if someone was already parked here? Could they leave?"

The young girl shrugged. "I don't know about that. Probably not, since it's so full of people. Did you want a dessert with that order?"

"No thanks. The sandwich sounds plenty." Derek closed the menu and smiled at her as he handed it to her. Better to be polite to people than demanding.

The question of parking could have implications for the crime scene. He could observe the logistics this Saturday since this year's Independence Day holiday fell on that day. Perhaps Megan would like to come also and make it a holiday for them both.

After a quick lunch, he walked next door to the four-year-old crime scene. The office was pleasantly cool after the hot pavement. The door chimed a bell sound as he walked in and looked around. A young woman in her twenties came out of an office on his right. She wore flip flops, shorts, and a tank top with a heavy sweater.

She asked, "Can I help you?"

"I wanted to speak to William Dunn."

She frowned. "Did you have an appointment?"

"No, I'm Detective Fielding. I'm working as a cold case investigator for the Sheriff's office." He showed her is badge and credentials. "I hoped to catch Mr. Dunn in."

"Oh, well, Uncle William is still at lunch. You can wait, I guess."

"Thanks, I would like to do so. Were you also working here four years ago when Adam Cranford was shot?"

Derek searched his memory for mention of office staff. He had not seen any notes on anyone.

"Yes, I'd been here about six months."

"Forgive me, but I don't recall your name in the notes."

"I'm Tammy Dunn. Uncle William is my dad's brother. I'm a receptionist and legal assistant, but I don't do the paralegal stuff. Uncle William hires someone freelance to do that if he needs it. He's what he calls a 'transactional attorney' and doesn't practice in court."

Derek asked, "So he's not continuing with the criminal law practice?"

Tammy rolled her eyes. "No, who would want to work with criminals? Uncle William does wills and trusts. He's an estate planning attorney."

Derek smiled. "That sounds much easier than going to court before a judge. I wonder if you could show me the room where the shooting happened while I'm waiting on your uncle?"

Tammy looked uncertain. "Do you need a warrant?"

"No, not if I'm given permission. Is it now your uncle's office?"

Tammy's brow cleared. "Oh, no, Uncle William kept his same office." She walked over to a closed door and turned the knob and threw the door wide. This is the room. It's really big, but we made it into a storage room. I sure didn't want to use it and neither did Uncle." Derek stepped into a very large room with windows covered in closed dusty blinds. The red-brick walls matched the bare brick floor. A desk had been shoved to one side and numerous white banker boxes sat on top of it. File cabinets lined another wall.

"We use it for storage of some of our current client's documents, but most of this was Mr. Cranford's paperwork. Uncle says the law requires we keep a deceased attorney's documents for five years or maybe seven in certain circumstances."

Derek suspected that was a direct quote from her uncle. He asked, "Where was the desk the night of the shooting?"

"At the back, under the windows. He sat with his back to the wall and the desk faced this door where we're standing. He had chairs in front of it that visitors could sit in then." She looked around, "It's pretty much like it was then, except the desk is pushed to one side. And we had the carpet taken out, because there were some blood stains on the carpet. Are you trying to find out who did it, again?
"Yes, do you have any suggestions?" Derek wondered

if Adam had been attracted to the young assistant. She was attractive but seemed indifferent to his passing.

"Nope. Haven't really thought about it much."

Derek raised his eyebrows. "Didn't you work for him?"

Tammy wrinkled her face. "Not if I could help it." Derek found Tammy's remarks quite intriguing. Any thoughts of a boss and employee romance were quickly fading. "You just worked for your uncle?"

"I was hired to work for both, but that Mr. Cranford just made me furious. He was always saying I made mistakes and telling his clients that the new girl wasn't very well-trained. When he thought I wasn't around, I heard him say that they hired me as a favor to his partner, and I wasn't very bright."

"So, he wasn't happy with your work?"

"My work was fine. Well, I make mistakes sometimes. But he often blamed his failure to do work for his clients on me. He would then gaslight me."

Derek knew the term but wanted to make sure how Tammy used it. "What do you mean by 'gaslight'?" "You know, like that movie where a man made his wife think she was crazy, so he could get her money. He would tell his clients I forgot to create a document or file it in the court. Then when I told him I did do it, he said I must have forgotten and was confused. Once I went and found the document and showed it to him. He said that he had done it. Grrrrr. I know I did it."

In a mastery of understatement, Derek said, "So you didn't like him?"

"Like him? I hated him. He was like a smiling snake. But don't think I killed him. I was at the concert."

"You attended the 4th of July fireworks concert?"

"Sort of. I was singing in the choral group in front of everyone until the fireworks started at 10:00 p.m. Then, we all went to a party at Freddie's parents' house once I found him in the crowd. He was my boyfriend. Now he's my fiancé."

Derek said, "So starting at 10:00 you started looking for Freddie. When did you find him?"

Tammy closed her eyes and thought. "It must have been about 10:30 p.m. just as the fireworks ended."

Derek stepped into Adam's former office. "Do you still use his computer?"

"No, the police took his laptop and never gave it back."

"Were you on an office network or was his separate?"

Tammy looked confused. "We use a network, but he took his laptop home with him often."

An intricate hand carved antique box caught Derek's attention on the desk. He stepped over and picked it up. "This is very nice. I'm surprised his wife didn't want to take it home." Tammy made a face. "That thing. It always stood on his desk right at the front where the visitors sat. He used to laugh and say that was his traveling file. Not that I ever saw him file things in it."

Derek looked at her. "It's too small to hold a regular size of paper without folding it, and it's locked."

Tammy said, "There's a key to it." She walked over to the desk and reached down to a top drawer. "Here's the key. I opened it once to see what was in it."

Derek took the key and turned it in the lock. "What is in it?"

"Just his passport. I guess that's why he said it was his traveling file."

"Did he travel a lot?"

"Not that I knew of."

"You didn't make any reservations for him?"

"No. He'd do it himself rather than ask me. I started gaslighting him too and pretending I didn't hear him."

Derek reflected that must have been a fun office for getting legal work done. He opened the wooden box and looked inside. Nothing was in the box. He said, "There's no passport in it now. Did his wife take it?"

Tammy peered into the box. "Not that I know of. The last time I looked, the passport was there. It must have been not long before he died in late June. He kept tapping it and smiling that snake smile. I wondered if he put something secret in it, but it was just the same passport."

As Derek held the box in his hand, he realized the interior was smaller than he expected. He closed the lid and then opened it again.

"Is there a drawer or other part of the box that opens?"

"Not that I know. It's real old. Mr. Cranford said it belonged to his great grandfather who was a bootlegger in the roaring twenties. Although, I'm not sure why they were roaring."

"They were 'roaring' because alcohol was illegal then, and people made their own and hid it from the police."

"Oh, well, I guess his great granddad made it. I don't think his family was as wealthy as his wife's. She's real nice. She's married to my uncle now. She brings me cookies on my birthday and tells me I'm doing a fine job and my uncle appreciates it."

Derek put to rest any suspicions of an office romance between Adam and Tammy, but she did remain a suspect. Like many people in this case, her life had improved for the better with the removal of Adam Cranford. Singing in a concert doesn't rule out quick breaks, and it sounded like she didn't meet up with the boyfriend right after the singing ended. He would need to find out when she left the stage. And of course, someone may have helped her.

The sound of the bell tinkling came through to them in Adam's office. He asked, "Did that front door make the same sound four years ago?"

"Yes, oh there's Uncle William. He can talk to you."

Chapter 5:
William Dunn, Esquire

Derek placed the wooden box back on the desk and followed Tammy into the entrance area. A tall and slender but fit man in his late forties stood just inside the door. He had light brown hair and a light-weight beige custom tailored suit with a tie.

"Hi, Uncle William. Here's a detective to see you."

William stepped forward to shake Derek's hand. "I've heard about you from Sheriff Tagger and also my wife."

Derek shook his hand and said, "Yes, I spoke to your wife earlier. I was hoping to catch you in your office this afternoon. I have some questions about the firm and the partnership."

"I'll do what I can to help. Why don't you come in and sit down?" William turned to Tammy, "Did you finish printing out copies of the will documents for Mrs. Benning to sign?"

"Yeah, sure I did. It's on the conference table."

"Why are you dressed like that? I told you we need to have professional attire when clients come, and you promised you would change."

"I was going to go home at lunch and change. Can I go now and take an extra half hour?"

"Yes, if it's all printed out."

Tammy nodded vigorously, tossed her winter sweater in her office before grabbing a purse and dashing out the door.

William ushered Derek into his office. Like Adam's it had red brick walls with tall windows and closed blinds through which sunlight filtered. A newer carpet covered the floor. His desk and the room were smaller than Adam's. A laptop sat on a neat desk with no open files lying around.

He closed the door and said, "Sorry about that. I don't normally criticize an employee in front of others, but today is important. I can't have her dressed for poolside when my oldest client is coming in."

Derek smiled slightly. "She did have a heavy sweater on to cover up partially."

William rolled his eyes showing a family resemblance to his niece. "She wouldn't need the sweater if she wore a jacket. Actually, Tammy is very clever. I suspect she knew I would ask her to go home and change. She had asked for today off, and I'd said no, not until tomorrow. Her fiancé is back in town this week."

"What does her fiancé do?"

"He just finished a four-year degree in something that I can't remember, maybe accounting? But he's back at his old summer job right now. He's an employee at the gun store just south of town and teaches firearm classes as well."

Derek nodded. Interesting combination. "I understand you have clients coming and don't want to delay you, but it would be helpful to learn more about Adam's law practice and what that entailed."

William shifted into his attorney personality and became cautious and precise. "Can you be more specific? That covers a wide range, and as you said, we have limited time. Also, I don't want to be accused of sour grapes."

Derek shifted more firmly into his homicide investigating personality. "Where exactly were you between 10:00 p.m. and 10:30 p.m. on July 4th four years ago?"

William raised his eyebrows. "Surely the police notes have that listed?"

Derek nodded, "They do, but I need a more specific answer."

William walked over to one window and slightly raised the blinds, letting in more light. "I was with my daughter who was 14 then. We usually go to the concert as it's become a family tradition, just the two of us. I thought it might be the last year as she would soon prefer to go with her friends in high school."

"Where exactly did you stand or sit at the concert?"

William shook his head. "I'm trying to remember. We've attended so many concerts over the years. I believe we parked down at the rec center, caught a shuttle, and sat down near the concert area. My niece was excited about being one of the singers that night. I wanted to be able to tell her I saw her."

"Did you separate from your daughter at any time?"

William gazed out the window. "She may have gone to the rest room at one point. I don't think I did, though." He turned back to look at Derek and smiled slightly. "Sorry, but I can't give you an airtight alibi, and I wish I could."

Derek asked, "Did you have a date that night? Or was it just you and your daughter? I understand your wife died many years ago?"

"I did not have a date. It was just my daughter and me. My wife died shortly after my daughter was born. She had cancer. She could have taken chemotherapy but that would have killed our child. She made a sacrifice. We hoped prayer would be sufficient. It wasn't."

"I'm sorry. I'm sure that was difficult."

"It was. That's when I came to appreciate Sharon. She and other ladies in the church were wonderful about stopping by to bring casseroles and check on us. The ladies were always willing to give advice. I knew nothing about babies. My mother came and stayed, but she had other family commitments. My father was an invalid, and her sister also had needs. Sharon was always sweet and kind. Never pushy but always willing to help if needed."

"How did you become a law partner with Adam?"

"I had just finished law school and passed the bar when my wife got pregnant. I didn't have much energy left for a law practice on my own after that, so I went into practice with an elderly lawyer who practiced estate planning. He died about six years ago, and I really missed sharing the expenses. Adam showed up one day and said he was looking for a partner as his criminal practice was getting too busy. I didn't really fall for that. Actually, he had landed himself in hot water because one of his clients was suing him for malpractice. I had established a good reputation for ethics and reliability."

"You saw through his maneuvering?"

William grinned. "Always. Adam didn't fool me. Maybe that's why he didn't bother me as much as others who felt tricked by him. I agreed to the partnership because it was better for me, too. I did insist on certain accounting practices and that I would only stick to transactional law. That suited him fine. So, he did his thing, and I did mine. We shared expenses on a building and both benefited from economies of cost. In other words, I didn't have to pay rent on my own, and we split any employee salaries."

Derek said, "That makes sense. What about his wife? Did you and Sharon ever deepen your relationship?"

"If you mean did we have an affair, the answer is no. Both of us are sincere in our Christian faith and would not have a relationship outside of marriage. Although I cared deeply for her, I would not say we really saw much of each other back then."

"So, you don't think Adam was jealous?"

"Adam? Jealous? I don't think so. He was an odd guy. If he felt injured, he would sneak around and get his own back, but he didn't argue or confront anyone. I just don't see him as that emotionally attached to people, even to his own family. He sort of lived in his own world, if that makes sense."

"Can you explain that?"

"He seemed to be mentally somewhere else much of the time. He was always the same, lukewarm. He never got really angry or happy or sad. He just always seemed placid and planning his next move."

"What about the law firm business? Was he poor at managing the finances?"

"No, he was very good at keeping records, paying

the bills, and showing a modest profit. We didn't get rich, but there was no missing money in our firm's IOLTA account if that's what you're wondering."

"By IOLTA you're referring to the trust fund that all lawyers must have to hold client funds until they are earned?"

"Yes, we formed an LLC, so it's run as a business with protected liability. The business had the IOLTA, and Adam's clients' funds were always carefully accounted for. I don't know about his personal life or business. I've heard he made some unwise decisions, but I didn't know much about it."

"Do you know who his clients were at the time of his death?"

William hesitated. "I can't reveal protected attorney/client information even though they weren't my clients, and the attorney is dead."

"I understand, but it would be helpful to know if one of them became angry with Adam. I know you all want this resolved and suspicions removed from the innocent."

"I do, but I can't go against ethical behavior to accomplish that."

That remark told Derek a great deal about the man sitting across the desk from him. "What about any boxes left in his office that would not reveal client secrets? What about financial records?"

William stood up. "Let's look. I haven't been in there in months. I have to keep it for legal reasons. I realize you could get a warrant, but not for the client privilege and I'm not that familiar with his papers. We just boxed up what the police did not take." The two men walked into Adam's office.

Derek asked, "Did you get his computer back?"

"No, I didn't need anything on it, and I forgot about it. I guess as a business asset I should have requested it back. I'm not sure if it still runs after this long."

"I can look in the evidence box for it and find out. What about that wooden box? Do you know much about it?"

William picked it up. "No, I think it's a Cranford family heirloom. I guess that's why Sharon didn't take it, and her children have never expressed an interest in his things."

"Was he not a good father?"

"Oooohhhh, I wouldn't say he was a bad father. From comments they've made since my marriage to Sharon, I gather he wasn't around much. Both their children are active in community events and always seemed to be doing things with friends. I think they did family outings to school plays, graduations, and church events but then went their own ways once there. If you're looking for a deep-seated hatred for a mean father, you won't find it with them. They seem very happy with their lives and marriages." William handed Derek the carved box. "You can certainly take this. I will write up a receipt for what I give you if you will sign it. No warrant needed for this. Here, let me give you an empty box to put things in."

"Thanks, I appreciate that." Derek carefully placed the possibly valuable antique in an empty banker's box. Several files labeled accounts receivable and such soon followed.

William said, "Now that we're in here I do remember going through his client files. Most of Adam's work was done in the criminal courts, and he would have been listed as the attorney of record on any open cases. They can be found by looking at the court records for that year."

"Thanks. By the way, I heard the bell on the outside door but did this door have one?"

"No. Adam usually kept it open, so he could see who came in."

"Was that typical for him to work at night?"

"Yes, some of his clients preferred to come then and some worked during the day. Also, he often spent his days doing county commission business."

"I understand you're now running for that seat."

"Yes, Freda is trying to turn our town into a giant shopping mall. She wants to replace these beautiful old buildings with condos and shops that she would get a commission on. She got into office by fighting a smelly chicken plant but then decided retail stores are perfectly fine no matter where they're located as long as she gets a commission."

Derek grinned. "She sounds like a character. I heard you had accused her of the murder. Was that just rhetoric or do you really believe it?"

William stopped looking in dusty boxes. "I said that because she accused me. I returned the favor by pointing out she had a stronger motivation as she couldn't get the job if Adam won, whereas I could get his wife if she divorced him." He looked at Derek and grinned. "If you could find her guilty, it would please me no end."

Derek smiled back. "We try to make sure the person arrested is actually guilty, sir."

William wiped the dust off his hands. "Adam didn't seem to consider guilt relevant. He would do anything to get someone off, yet others he didn't seem to try hard. Not sure why."

"From what I've heard about Mr. Cranford, I can definitely say that I have a different approach."

Chapter 6:
Unlocking the Past

Derek carried the banker's box out to his SUV and traveled a block or two to his temporary office. He met Tagger in the hallway.

"Are you moving in, Fielding?"

"Not I. Adam Cranford's things."

"I thought we had all that."

"There were a few things left behind I'd like to look at."

"I'll check on you later. I wanted to ask you something when I'm free." Tagger continued walking.

Derek agreed and unlocked his office door. During the day he did not want to carry the evidence back to the lockup room. He set the box on his desk and pulled out the wooden box. It intrigued him. He sat down at his desk chair and shook it. Nothing rattled.

He brought his computer back to life and searched online for a similar antique box. He noticed the time was getting late. He had about an hour before he left for home. His search soon rewarded him. He didn't find the exact box, but an article told him about hidden compartments in antique lock boxes of the late 19th and early 20th century.

He soon sat back in his chair and twisted the box in his hands. Nothing showed a crack or a hinge. He picked up his cell phone and turned on the magnifying glass app. There might be something at the bottom. He pressed and pulled but nothing happened.

Sheriff Tagger opened the door. "Have you got a minute? What is that?"

"This is what stayed on Adam's desk all the time and what he called his 'traveling file,' although he didn't travel."

Tagger pulled up a chair and looked closer. "It's really old."

"Supposedly it was his great grandfather's handmade box. Said relative was a bootlegger."

"Mmmmm. I've heard tales about Adam's ancestors. Was anything in it?"

"Nothing, but Tammy said he kept his passport in it at one time." Derek continued to twist the box and pull on some of the carvings.

"Maybe it was just wishful thinking then?" "He doesn't sound like a whimsical man, but rather one who planned ahead."

Derek glanced at the screen again and set the box down. "I wonder if there's a false bottom in it through the top." He pressed on the inner compartment and then at each corner. Suddenly a drawer on the bottom popped open.

"Well!" exclaimed Sheriff Tagger. "Who would have expected that? I thought you were regressing to grammar school when we kids had hunts for secret treasure in haunted houses."

Derek laughed. "It is kind of fun. Let's see what we have."

He pulled the drawer that had popped open all the way out and tried to reach his fingers in. "There's paper and something else, but I can't quite get them." He turned the box upside down and a key with a folded piece of paper slid out."

Tagger shook his head. "I can't believe it. My officers missed this, and it's been sitting there all this time."

"It's not something a crime scene tech would normally look for. Speaking of which, I think we need to get these tested before we handle them."

"Good idea, but I'd like to see what they are first. Here, I'll get some gloves and an evidence bag." Tagger disappeared out the door as Derek gently shook the paper free of the box. He used the box to press open the folded paper–a photocopy of an airline ticket dated for July 10th four years ago. Maybe Adam was planning on traveling, after all.

Tagger returned with gloves and an evidence bag. "What is that? A one-way ticket to the Cayman Islands? Really? Adam was leaving town?"

"Looks like it." Derek slid the paper into one bag and the key into another bag. "Do you recognize the key? It seems to be a safety deposit box. Is it one for your local bank on the corner of the square?"

Tagger held up the bag. "No, it's not. I know their numbering system. I agree it's a safety deposit box key from the number printed on it. Hopefully we'll find a reference in that box you carried in or already in evidence."

Derek sat back in his chair and said, "It's odd this is not the actual ticket but just a copy of it."

"Maybe the original ticket is in some of his other

things. I've heard Adam kept good records, part of being an attorney, I guess." Tagger looked at his watch. "I got so excited at your find I forgot to mention why I came in here. My wife's sister owns a B&B here in town and she wanted to know if you and Megan want to stay free of charge this week to save on the long commute? She's normally full for the holiday but had a cancellation."

"I don't know that Megan can during the week. Her job location would require a long commute, but let me talk to her about this Friday and over the weekend? Does your sister-in-law need an answer now?"

"No, I'll let her know you need to speak to your wife. I'm going to ask for a quick turn around on testing these for fingerprints and other trace evidence, but it might take a while. I would give them the box but after four years and everyone handling it, I don't see it as reliable."

"The secret compartment might yield something, but what about the key? If I find where it goes, we need to get a warrant and open it."

Tagger nodded. "Yes, I think we only need to dust it for prints since it's metal, and we can't wait weeks to find a safety deposit box. Who knows? After this long, it may be about to expire or expired with no yearly payments. Time is of the essence."

Derek agreed that time was of the essence for the key but also to get home for dinner. Megan had told him she was trying a new recipe. Neither of them cooked often, and he didn't want her to think he forgot. He glanced at the time again and said quickly, "I haven't looked at Adam's laptop yet. I'm hoping if it's plugged in that it will work, even if the battery is dead.

Do you know if the techs found anything helpful on it?"

"They said they didn't find anything."

"I'll take a look tomorrow. I need to get this locked up for the night and head back to Atlanta."

Tagger nodded and said, "I knew I was right to hire you. First day and you're finding secret compartments in old boxes." He held the evidence bags and walked away laughing. "Maybe we can start a treasure hunt department too!"

Derek grinned as he finished locking up, returned the items to the evidence room, and then left for his long drive back to Atlanta. Staying in town for a few days would be nice, but he wouldn't want to leave Megan. Still, it was a nice sense of accomplishment to find a clue on his first day. He wondered what that key would open.

Megan wondered, too, after he told her about it. She grinned and said, "What if it unlocks his great grandfather's secret moonshine recipe?"

Derek smiled back. "As long as no one's using it, that's fine. Otherwise, we'll let the ATF know. They handle illegal liquor operations."

Megan said, "Fortunately, no moonshine or white lightening or whatever it was called back then. We are having baked chicken in a sauce of basil and tomatoes. This one was easy. I just followed the recipe for combining everything and putting it in the oven."

Derek moved his phone and laptop from the table to his office desk. "Sounds great and smells delicious. By the way I wanted to ask you something." Derek mentioned Taggers offer of a free place to stay. "I know you can't do it during the week, and I don't want to stay on my own, but if you're off on Friday we could go up then."

Megan sat down at the table and sipped a glass of tea. "You know what. That might work out well. I haven't had a chance to mention it, but that little article I'm writing is turning into a big issue. I may need to travel out West for a day or two."

"Oh? Why is that?" Derek also poured a glass of tea and sat down across from her at the kitchen table.

"The state legislature is holding a vote on whether to limit what a church can do with its land or buying new land. Depending on the wording, that could be a huge violation of religious rights. I'd like to interview those representatives for and against and actually be at the vote. It's live-streamed, but I'd rather see for myself what goes on off camera. I can also catch people as they come or go." She sipped her tea. "If I flew out early tomorrow morning, then I could get in place for the vote, spend the night, and have time to catch everyone. I could fly back the following day. It would help in case the vote is delayed also."

Derek said, "In that case, if you're gone, I could stay at the Lahillsville B&B tomorrow night and maybe the next. I'll offer to pay her. Do you want to come up for the weekend?"

"Yes. I'd love it. I'm off on Friday. I'd like to look at the murder scene or at least the building. It's the same time of year and same holiday, isn't it?" "Yes, that will help me get an idea of the logistics. I still can't figure out how no one saw anyone come and go out of his building. We'll do a reconstruction and see if we can get an insight into the ambiance and location better this weekend."

Megan put on her oven mitts. She glanced at

Derek, "But without the murder."
Derek winced. "Without the murder."

Chapter 7:
Nothing There To See

Derek texted his plans to Tagger and packed a suitcase. He was eager to pursue yesterday's leads. Parting with Megan may be sweet sorrow today, but they had a happy reunion to look forward to later in the week. His first action after checking out the evidence boxes was to search for Adam's laptop.

He found it at the bottom of the largest box. He pulled out a slim and expensive laptop sealed in plastic with the tech's note: "Nothing found." Below that was the username and password to access the computer.

Derek opened the laptop, found its cord and plugged it into an electrical socket. He looked for more notes from the tech but couldn't find any. He opened the computer to see if any notes were attached to the keyboard. No. That was odd. In his experience, a forensic examination of a laptop resulted in lists of what was found and any suspicious files or activities.

He looked through the other files and plastic bags in the evidence box. Nothing related to the computer although he did find some bank account information that he set aside. Computers were not his forte, but he could read, so he booted up the laptop hoping it didn't need a charged battery to work. It didn't, and he entered the codes to see it come to life. He soon realized with dismay the words "nothing found" were literal and not an expert assessment of criminal content.

The screen showed only the photo of that year's operating system edition. No software, no files, nothing. He looked in the Documents folder and through the disk drives, but there were no files. He found no installed software, which was odd, because certain software came with this type of computer. It had all been erased. He sat back and thought.

The first question was chain of custody. Did this happen at Adam's office or after the police took charge of it? Was this the killer or someone else? Then followed the last question: why?

Derek pushed his chair back, locked his door, and walked to Tagger's office where he fortunately found him. "Do you have a moment?"

"Yes, a moment, I've got a meeting shortly. A problem?"

"Yes. A big one. Did you or any of your officers ever look at Adam's computer?"

Tagger frowned and looked down at his desk thinking. "I didn't. I'm not into that stuff. As I recall the techs bagged it and sent it to the IT lab the state runs. Why? Did you find something we missed?"

"Did you think it was odd the techs just said, 'nothing found.'"

Tagger frowned again. "Spit it out man. What's the problem? If nothing was found, I didn't pursue it. What have you found?"

"Nothing."

"If you're being funny...."

"There's nothing on the computer. Someone has

completely erased every file and every software program from it. So, several questions arise. First, is this really Adam's computer? Second, was this done while it was in his office before the techs took it? Third, could it have been done intentionally or accidentally here or at our labs? I looked at the properties part of the disk drive, and it was erased very early in the morning on July 5th. I've never known dead men to erase their computers, unless it could be programed ahead of time."

Tagger stared at Derek until comprehension hit. "*Nothing* doesn't mean no evidence found but nothing on the darn thing."

"Correct."

"I don't want to insult, but are you sure you turned it on correctly?"

Derek raised his eyebrows. "Perhaps you would like to look?"

Tagger glanced at a clock on his wall and jumped up to follow Derek down the hall and the quickly unlocked door. He looked at the note and then the computer. He tried a few keys and slid the mouse around. He said a few words he wouldn't say in public. "I know the officers who secured the scene. The lab techs I don't know, but they were from out of the county and experts. This doesn't look like an accident. It's just too empty."

Derek sat down. "The question is can the erased data be recovered? I know sometimes it can be under certain circumstances, but I don't know about this."

Tagger sat down in the guest chair and ran his hand down his face. "Bother! I should have caught this. It came back several weeks later with the tag 'nothing found'. No one in local law enforcement has forensic IT skills. Let me check with the state and the GBI and see if they can recover it. Although, there may be a conflict of interest, if it was their fault in the first place. What a mess."

Derek nodded. "What about the key I found? If they've finished testing for prints, I could call banks and at least check to see about their numbering system before visiting them."

Tagger nodded. "I'll check. Let you know soon." He didn't slam the door because he left it open on his angry rush out of the office.

Derek pulled the file he had found with the bank records. Then he looked at the time. He still needed to interview Freda Faulkner while she was in her office this morning. He would need to leave soon but still had time. The bank records became interesting. One account was an IOLTA account in just Adam's name, and it was at a different bank than their current one. Why did he keep his own IOLTA account? Why was it at a bank in a different town in the county? Derek would ask for a warrant for the bank to get a copy of all Adam's accounts there. He set that in progress and then left the building.

His first stop was to the B&B where he left his bag and met the owner. Mrs. Tagger's sister was named Louise. She was a businesslike woman who said, "I appreciate your offer to pay, but I'd like to do something to help. My sister and her husband have put up with a lot of insults over the years from people who think Tagger didn't want to find the killer or worse."

Derek said, "That's kind of you, and we would appreciate it. I'm sure the Tagger's do also. My wife is traveling. She can stay over the weekend, but it will just be me for tonight."

Louise smiled. "The Sheriff says you two are newlyweds. Ironically, it's our suite we normally use for newlyweds that's open so you might tell her that."

Derek smiled back, "I will. Her name is Megan."

"I've got that down on the reservation. Now follow me, and I'll show you to the room. You can leave your things there, or we have a safe at the reception desk. We use old fashioned keys. But if someone 'forgets' to return one then we rekey the lock."

Derek followed Louise up a flight of stairs. "That's good to know. I guess the 4th of July is your busiest time of year with the fireworks concert?"

"Pretty much. I remember the night that Adam got himself killed. It was real busy and hot too. I wondered if he stayed in his office because they had that new air conditioner. He was getting a little old to be out in this humidity."

Derek said, "Have they always kept it so cool in there?"

"Adam did, and William hasn't changed it."

Derek wondered. If that was well known, could someone have sought a cool place out of the heat and humidity? They then discovered Adam counting his money? The money under the body didn't mean there hadn't been more. As with the computer, it might be a question of what had been there. He would have to investigate that possibility.

Chapter 8:
Freda Faulkner

Derek left the Lahillsville B&B and drove another two blocks to Freda Faulkner's office. It was on the same side as Adam's building but a block away. Large red and white signs proclaimed her candidacy for county commissioner. Interesting that William did not have any on his building. Maybe he would. An even larger sign declared the building to be the location of the Faulkner Real Estate Agency.

Derek parked in front of the building in one of several spaces available. Apparently, this was not their busy time of day or year. He opened the door and walked in. A young man sat at the reception desk and asked if he could help him. Derek showed his credentials and asked for Ms. Faulkner.

The receptionist stared at him. "I..I..don't know. She's here but let me check." The young man walked down the hall and returned following a woman wearing a stylish business suit. Her streaked hair was carefully dyed and styled to cover any possible grey strands.

"I'm Freda Faulkner, Detective Fielding. I would have preferred an appointment, but I don't have any house showings today. We're slow right now. Most people are on vacation. I just happened to be here. Why don't you come on back?"

Derek listened to the flow of conversation. He didn't try to interrupt or rush her. He said, "I'm glad you can fit me in then, Ms. Faulkner."

She waved her hand carelessly. "Oh, call me Freda. Everyone else does. When you're in both sales and politics you can't be too formal."

Derek followed her down the hall into a conference room. He sat in the seat she pointed to on one side of a large table while she took another chair opposite him. He said, "I understand you're up for re-election this year."

"Yes, William is running against me. He's still living in the past and wants to keep everything as it is with no progress at all."

"I thought you were the one against progress since you were so adamantly against the chicken processing plant four years ago before the developers withdrew their offer."

Freda waved her hand again as though swatting a fly. "That was different. That would have made the land unsellable and run off tourists. Adam knew that. He promoted it because he was making a nice kickback on the side."

"Do you have proof of that kickback?"
"Proof? Not anything in writing, if that's what you mean."

"Then why do you think he accepted a bribe?"

"Because the secretary that works for the county development office told me she heard the owners whispering and talking low with Adam one time when they came up to look at the property. She stepped closer behind a partition, so she could hear and heard them mention the thousands he could derive from a finder's fee." Freda snorted. "Finder's fee, my eye. That would be an illegal bribe."

Derek nodded. A whispered conversation heard by an eavesdropper repeated to a political opponent was not very reliable and not admissible in court since it would also be hearsay. Nonetheless, he found it believable. "So, you decided to run and get the plant stopped before they started to build."

Freda grinned. "Darn right. Those out-of-state owners wouldn't be the ones living here and putting up with the stench and the wear and tear on our roads from constant truck traffic."

Derek tossed in a little jab to try and pierce Freda's self-complacency. "Adam's death was fortuitous for you. You won his seat and stopped the plant."

Freda was not fazed. She had become a seasoned politician as well as a successful saleswoman. "The whole county benefited from his death, especially, his partner. I'm sure he did it. I hope you arrest him."

"We need proof to make arrests. Do you have any evidence that he did it?"

Freda sighed. "Just my instincts."

"I've read your statement, but I'm not clear where you were that night from 10:30 p.m. to 11:30 p.m. It says you were wandering around 'working the crowd' and asking for people to sign your petition."

"That's what I was doing."

"What part of the crowd between those hours?"

Freda waved her hand again swatting away an irrelevancy. "I have no idea. I just walked around and chatted. The fireworks were always to the north of me, so I never left the viewing area."

"Not even to stop at the rest rooms or come back to your office?"

"I might have, but it's been a long time, and I don't remember." She leaned forward, "I can't say I'm sorry he's dead, but I didn't do it. I'd look closer to home if I were you."

"Can you be more specific?"

"His wife or his partner. Either one would be happy to see him gone. Sharon must have really been furious to sign my petition. I was shocked. I was just needling her when I asked. Appearances are everything to that family, and I sure didn't expect her to respond." She leaned back. "I'd look at Sharon or William, preferably him."

"Have you ever seen Sharon with a gun in her hand that indicates she knows how to use one?" Freda gazed up to the ceiling. "Actually, I have. We have turkey shoots every Thanksgiving to benefit the youth foundation. We don't actually shoot turkeys, of course. We sell tickets for people to shoot at targets in a contest, and the winner gets a store-bought turkey. Sharon's bought some tickets and shot several years."

"Did she win any prizes?"

"Mmmmm. I don't recall her winning anything, but she does know how to shoot. And William can too. He goes hunting or at least he did when he was young before his wife died."

"And do you know how to use a gun?"

Freda smiled. "Yes. I've been at the charity shoots also. Good community relations. But I didn't win any prizes either."

Derek did not remember a report that her gun was tested. Both William and Sharon had handguns that passed inspection. He said, "Did the police take your gun for testing?"

"No, they didn't."

"Do you still have it?"

"No, I traded it in for a better model not long after the murder. If people were coming in shooting us business owners, I wanted to be prepared."

"Who did you sell it to?"

"The gun store south of town. It's called the 2nd Amendment store."

"Can you find a receipt for that transaction?"

Freda shrugged. "I'll look, but it was a personal sell, not business. I don't keep any papers that don't need to be listed on my taxes. I have too much paper as it is in this business."

"Do you know the serial number of the gun and the caliber?"

Freda gazed at him a moment, "Are you seriously thinking I would shoot Adam, that slimy weasel?"

"One of the purposes of my investigation is to stop baseless accusations and save reputations. So, testing your gun would help eliminate you. Having a witness where you were during the hours I've mentioned would help also."

"I had a Glock 19. It used 9 mm bullets, but I have no idea what the serial number was. I can't imagine why I would have kept records, but I'll look."

"Do you remember the exact date you sold it?"

"Not long after Adam was shot. I wanted a larger gun. I'd say maybe that September sometime."

Freda arched her eyebrows and leaned back slightly, "But if you're looking for a suspect who can shoot, have you spoken to the mayor?"

"Why would I speak to him?"

"He's married to Sharon's sister but more importantly, he hated Adam. I've often wondered if Adam had something over him because Mayor Andrew always supported Adam's schemes for the town. Yet, I've seen him glaring at Adam behind his back."

"What type of schemes?"

"Keeping the downtown where Adam's office was located undeveloped and unchanged with that same old 1880s look of boring red brick."

Derek raised his eyebrows, "And you want to develop it?"

"Someone needs to. I'm surprised those old buildings haven't fallen down with the neglect the town inflicts due to lack of maintenance. They need to take off restrictions on preserving historical accuracy and get in some new businesses."

"Such as?"

"Tear 'em down and put in a bunch of condos above some upscale boutiques. It would pull in the Atlanta weekend visitors."

Derek reflected the mayor may have other reasons for agreeing with Adam if he preferred a quiet and sleepy town.

Freda continued, "And moreover, he doesn't have an alibi. I was working the crowd and meeting people but not him."

"He was not up for re-election that year?"

"He was, but Andrew is very good at avoiding any citizen that might ask him a question, or even worse, ask him to do something. So, he just appears on stage for a speech and then quickly disappears. Don't know what happened to him after his speech kicking off the concert. He wasn't greeting people like I was."

Derek thanked Freda and left. He wasn't sure how much value to assign to Freda's criticism of the mayor, but he was Sharon's brother-in-law, and could help answer some questions. He had planned to interview both the mayor and his wife anyway, but he would move them up in priority on his list.

Also, added to his list was a visit to the gun store. It would be nice to have a warrant first if he could get one. He was doubtful, without more evidence, that Freda was involved. On the other hand, he would like to meet Tammy's fiancé who worked with guns at that store and probably was a good enough marksman to shoot a man in the center of the forehead 50 feet away.

Derek looked up the store's address and drove a few miles through open countryside to a fenced-in building with a shooting range behind it. He went inside to find a man in his twenties with very short hair and a buff physique. Derek introduced himself and showed his credentials. "Are you Freddie, by any chance?"

The young man did not look surprised that Derek knew his name. He said, "Yes."

Derek waited but the man said nothing else. "I believe you must be Tammy Dunn's fiancé? Is that right?"

"Yes."

"As you may know, the Sheriff's department has reopened the cold case of Adam Cranford's murder. Tammy tells me she was with you after her singing ended at the concert."

Freddie crossed his arms and looked back at Derek, neither defensively or curiously. "That's correct. She was."

"Can you tell me what time you met her and left for your parents' house?"

Freddie was silent for a moment and said, "About 15 minutes after the fireworks ended. That would have been about 10:45 or 11:00 p.m.."

"Did you see her before that time?"

"Yes, she was on stage."

"Did the singers take breaks or did she meet with you before then?"

"No, that was the busy time."

"What about yourself? Where were you during the 10:30 p.m to 11:00 p.m. time?"

"Why do you care?"

"I'm getting a clear picture of who was where."

"If you're going to ask about my whereabouts, I'll get a lawyer."

"You can do that, but I'm not bringing you in for questioning."

"Still, I'll get a lawyer with me before I'll say anything else."

Derek nodded. "We can do that. Please call the Sheriff's department to make an appointment as soon as possible. Otherwise, I would need to bring you in for questioning at my convenience." Freddie did not react. He stared back at Derek and nodded, his arms still crossed over his chest.

Derek said, "I do have another question that doesn't involve yourself. Freda Faulkner tells me she traded a gun with your shop the September after the murder. Can you tell me where that gun is now?"

"I was back at college in September, but I'll ask the owner, Mr. Hibbard." Freddie walked to the back of the store and through a door marked "Private." Mr. Hibbard appeared a few minutes later. He was an older man who had the look of a retired soldier with stiff posture and piercing eyes.

"I'm Howard Hibbard. How can I help you?"

Derek again introduced himself and showed his credentials. "I'm trying to locate a gun that Freda Faulkner traded in with you in September four years ago. She says it was a Glock 19. I don't have the serial number, but I need to follow up on some leads that were not pursued then." Derek hoped he could eliminate speculation that Freda was a hot suspect, and he merely needed documentation.

Howard smiled. "I'm always glad to help law enforcement. We support them here." He winked. "I won't even ask for a warrant. Let me see what I can find on the computer." He sat down on a stool and turned a computer monitor towards himself. "Freddie, can you help that man who just walked in the store?"

Freddie left and was no longer staring over Howard's shoulder. "Let's see, four years ago. I do keep most transactions. Here it is. She traded in her Glock and got a Sig Sauer. The gun was resold to an Eric Smith from an Atlanta address, and he passed our background checks. I'll write this down for you."

"Can you also write down the serial number?"

"Glad to." Howard wrote down the information and handed it over to Derek. "I don't know if you're looking for free advice, but if you think Freda could actually hit a target, especially a man, from even one foot away, think again."

Derek smiled. "A bad shot?"

"Very bad. Lucky shots do happen, but not dead center in the forehead as I heard about Adam's murder."

"What about your assistant, Freddie? Is he a good shot?"

Howard smiled, "Yeah, he is, but accounting majors who want a career in forensic accounting with the FBI often are good with guns."

"I see. Thanks for the help and the information." He smiled, "I wish everyone was as helpful as you have been."

"I wanted to go into law enforcement when I got out of the army many years ago, but it just didn't work out. Still, I can make sure people are trained to protect themselves with this store."

Derek nodded and left, folding and putting the paper in his pocket. Freddie was probably overly influenced by his studies by insisting on a lawyer, unless he did shoot Adam. It had happened that those attracted to law enforcement were themselves criminals. But he doubted Howard would have kept someone with those tendencies employed for this many years. As for Freda, he only had Howard's word on it, but she might not have been able to shoot with such deadly accuracy. But then no one in this case, except Freddie, seemed to have that skill. It was one thing to hit someone, another to hit the dead center of the forehead just once, standing 50 feet away.

Chapter 9:
Hidden Treasure

Derek returned to his SUV. He noticed a text from Tagger requesting he stop by his office. He drove back to town and was soon seated in front of Tagger's desk.

"Hello, Fielding. You asked for a warrant before you left, but our judges like to know who they're dealing with, so I had to intervene. We have a warrant to get Adam's bank account or accounts at State Bank."

Derek smiled. "Not how I've done it in Atlanta, but I'll remember for the future."

Tagger also smiled, "And even better news, the key only had Adam's prints or partial prints so we can go on a treasure hunt."

"We?"

"Yes, I want to go to the bank as well. The number is within its range. Since this bank is still in our county, although barely, I have jurisdiction. Let's go."

Derek collected the information he had on Adam's account at that bank and joined Tagger in his patrol car. Derek said, "If they do have the safety deposit box, then we'll need another warrant just for it."

"I know, but it will help to know if that is where it's located. If so, it would be part of his probate estate, and Sharon was his executor. She could let us in without a warrant, if she wants to."

"Do you think she would do so?"

Tagger tapped his fingers on the steering wheel. "I think so. Of course, if I tell her about it and she refuses, she could still access it as executor and walk off with the contents before we can get a warrant."

Derek said, "Did Adam have a safety deposit box at the local bank on the square?"

"Yes, he did, that's why I was surprised he had another one." Tagger continued to drive and listen to the police calls in the background. Neither man said anything else until they reached the large State Bank branch and parked in front of it. Derek reflected that a treasure hunt may have appealed to Tagger, but so did righting any mistakes he'd made as a new Sheriff.

After presenting the warrant and their credentials, they met Ms. Forsythe, the bank manager, a woman of about 60 with short cropped grey hair. She read over their warrant and said, "I'll be glad to help you. Let me look at our computer." She entered keystrokes on a monitor with a privacy screen and finally said. "Mr. Cranford has two accounts here. He has an attorney's IOLTA account and a savings account. But this is rather odd, very odd indeed."

"How is that?" asked Tagger.

"We have it set up to cancel an account if there is no activity for six months. But he has set his accounts to automatically deposit money each month back and forth."

"What do you mean?" asked Derek.

"The IOLTA account automatically transfers $25 into the savings every other month. The savings account automatically transfers $25 into the IOLTA the other month. I'm not sure why he would want to do that."

"Your software would not pick that up?"

"Not unless there is no activity."

"So, it could go on forever?" asked Derek.

"Oh, no, it would run out of money eventually. Each year $50.00 is taken out of his savings to pay for his safe deposit box and once he ran out of money it would trigger us. Since he has $500 in savings that would take several years."

Tagger said, "A safe deposit box? Is this the key for it?"

Ms. Forsythe looked at the key handed to her and typed into her computer. She handed it back and said, "That's his numbered box account. I can't let you in without a different warrant, though."

"I understand. Can you give us printouts of the accounts our warrants do cover?"

"Yes, how far back do you want them?"

"How far do they go?"

"Twenty years but only the last five are on my computer. I'd need to request the others from our documents department."

"If you could do that and also give us what you have that would be a help."

"I'll go back to when he had five million dollars in each, and I can print it out."

Tagger looked stunned. "Million? He had a total of ten million dollars, including the IOLTA account?"

"Yes, but as I say that changed about four years ago. It looks like on July 5th all but $500.00 was transferred to an offshore account he had maintained in the Cayman Islands for several years."

Tagger repeated. "Cayman Islands? For several years? But he didn't travel."

"But he planned," said Derek.

"Not very well, since he's dead," growled Tagger.

While Ms. Forsythe left to retrieve their documents, Tagger said, "I've run into this before. Getting a warrant for a deceased person's safety deposit box is more difficult because it now belongs to the heirs. I think I'm going to take a chance and ask Sharon if she will come open it and let us take what we find. If she will sign permission, we don't need the warrant."

Derek didn't comment. It was Tagger's decision.

Tagger called Sharon and explained the situation. "I know you were Adam's executor, and this could help clear up the mystery. It would be the same as his other box......I know probate is closed, but you still just need proof you were the executor and his death certificate....Yes, I'll wait."

Tagger looked at Derek. "She's calling William to ask his opinion on their house phone."

Derek nodded. Based on his interviews with both, he expected to see them both at the bank shortly.

He was right. Sharon and William arrived together, presented the proper documents to Ms. Forsythe who then showed them into the safety deposit box area and used the bank key with Tagger's key to open a large box. She backed away and said, "I'll leave you all alone. Let me know when you're finished."

Sharon smiled and thanked her. She looked up at Tagger. "It's your show, Sheriff. Open the box."

Tagger did look like he'd found a treasure and slowly opened the box. They all gasped. Stacks of hundred-dollar bills lined one half of the box. The other held three handguns in plastic bags and a document folder. "Will you sign a release for me to take these items into evidence for processing, Ms. Dunn?"

Sharon said, "Where did all that money come from? Was Adam hiding it from me? Oh, yes, of course, you can take it, but I would like the money back if it's honestly come by."

William said, "We need to know how much is there, but I realize you may need to fingerprint it first. Also, can we itemize the documents and get the serial numbers of the guns?"

Tagger said, "Yes, I have some evidence gloves in my car."

Derek felt in his coat pocket, "Actually I brought a pair. Allow me." He counted the money in front of the others. "I count $5,000.00 even. Here's the serial numbers of the two guns." Derek read off the numbers while William wrote them down and then turned around a sheet of paper for both Sharon and Sheriff Tagger to sign."

Tagger looked around him. "I need something to carry all this in. I can't walk out of here with handfuls of cash."

Sharon reached in her purse and pulled out a plastic bag. "I use it in case of accidents with the toddlers, but don't worry it's new and clean."

As Adam's executor, Sharon closed out the other accounts and did take that money with her. She said she would need to find out if that was really client funds in the IOLTA.

Derek left the building reflecting that Sheriff Tagger had found his treasure, but he was still looking for a killer.

As Tagger drove them back to town, Derek asked, "What about Adam's laptop? Have you found out if the lab is able to recover the data?"

"That's turning into a fiasco. It looks like the GBI is backed up for months."

"What about a private lab?"

"I guess we could, but the cost would be way above my budget."

"Megan has a friend named Lisa who owns a computer company in Atlanta. One of her company's services is to recover lost data on damaged disk drives and from hacked computers. I could check with her. She might keep the costs reasonable."

"Sure. Go ahead."

Derek found Lisa's number and called. "Lisa, this is Derek Fielding, do you have a moment?"

Lisa exclaimed in her cheerful voice, "Problems already! Well, if you're calling for marital advice, be aware I'll always take Megan's side."

Derek laughed. "Nothing like that. I wanted to know if your company can retrieve erased data on a laptop hard drive?"

"Possibly. Tell me more."

Derek did. He put Lisa on speaker phone and introduced Sheriff Tagger. He explained the problem and the need for confidentiality and chain of custody.

Lisa said, "I'm familiar with law enforcement needs. We've done work for some of the attorneys in the city and around the state. From what you say, I think we can retrieve some, if not all, of it. It really depends on if it was a factory reset or a command to erase data."

"How would I find that out?"

"Let me look at it, and I'll tell you."

Sheriff Tagger asked, "How much do you charge? We have a limited budget."

"I'll charge nothing to look at it. Then I can let you know what I can do and a quote to go with it."

"Sounds fine," said Tagger.

"How do you want to get it to me?"

Derek said, "I'm coming back tomorrow. Megan is on assignment out of state and will return tomorrow afternoon if all goes well. Why don't I bring it down to you when I meet her?"

"That sounds fine; I can take time to look at it. Are you all leaving town again?"

"Yes, Megan's joining me here for the 4th of July festival and holiday."

"Sounds lovely. Let me know when to expect you tomorrow."

"Will do." Derek hung up.

Tagger said, "That would be a miracle if she could recover the data. I was expecting months, if even then."

"Lisa's firm has a good reputation. She's helped Megan solve some mysteries. I'm sure she knows what to look for on the computer."

Tagger said, "Another treasure hunt. I hope this one is as successful. Where are you on the interviews we discussed?"

Derek explained his results with Freda and Freddie.

Tagger laughed. "Test Freda's gun? I didn't think to do that. One reason is I've seen her shoot at those Turkey contests each Thanksgiving."

"Can't hit the target?"

"Oh, she can hit a target, just not her own. I guess she could have accidentally hit something. I have known her all my life. I can't see her trying to physically harm someone. She expresses her anger in words and talking."

"I'll try to find the man who bought her gun tomorrow. Since you have the bullet, we can match the results."

"I suppose. Why are you suspicious of Freddie? That will take up more time if he shows up with an attorney."

"Mainly because of his marksmanship. The more I think of the fact that only one shot was fired, and it was dead center tells me the shooter had to be very skilled."

"I've wondered about that, too. The only people I know remotely concerned with this case who have those skills are some of the people who hunt or practice at a shooting range."

"Would a hunter have those skills? A hunter would normally use a rifle not a handgun."

Tagger looked startled. "Good point. Military? Up close fighting?"

"Yes, I'd look at any trained military or law enforcement including undercover types such as FBI or CIA."

"I don't know of anyone around here who fits that description unless it's in their background and not recent."

"Could be." Tagger grinned. "It definitely doesn't fit Freda. She couldn't keep from telling everyone she's a spy for more than five minutes."

Derek also smiled. "She's not at the top of my list.

What do you think of her comments on Mayor Andrew?"

"Anything's possible, but Andrew's more of an avoidance problem kind of guy, like Adam. I can't see him taking that kind of decisive action. Certainly not on behalf of his wife's sister."

"Blackmail?"

"Maybe. Or maybe Freda would like to sling some mud because she wants to develop the downtown, and Andrew is against it."

"Still, I'll move him and his wife up on my interview list."

Chapter 10:
Adam Michael Cranford, Jr.

Derek worked late that afternoon, checking the backgrounds and history of several people around or near the case but not finding anyone with superior shooting or hunting skills. He looked through the court records to get a list of Adam's criminal clients at the time of his death. He also kept an eye on his cell phone. He and Megan had texted when each had an opportunity that day. He didn't want to miss another from her.

Finally, he pulled out the stack of documents from State Bank and started going through the past five years. As the bank manager had said, for the last four years it was simply month after month of reverse transfers and a yearly automatic withdrawal to pay for the safety deposit box fee.

However, going further back than four years told an interesting tale. The IOLTA account showed frequent cash deposits. Derek frowned. Why were Adam's clients paying in cash? Not a single check or ACH deposit. Were these clients? There were no withdrawals except to transfer to his savings account every few months. The amounts totaled up to millions over time but not in large enough amounts to trigger required reporting to the government. Sometime before the past five years, Adam had begun transferring money to an account in the Cayman Islands in low amounts. The last transfer was the early morning after his death in one large amount.

Derek sat back and considered the situation. If Adam was hiding money from his wife, then putting it in the IOLTA would make sense. Any divorce settlement would not include client money. If the intent was to hide it from the IRS, then it became more problematic. His savings account would have been reported and the IOLTA for the business. Derek looked through Adam's tax returns. The money was not reported. Derek looked closer at the savings account. It was in Adam Cranford's name but with a different middle initial. Adam was Adam M. and this was Adam N. Further research showed that the savings was originally his father's account. His father still paid taxes on it. His father died over twenty years ago. They were a remarkably lively family after death.

Derek sighed. He was not a forensic accountant. Freddie had chosen his career well. From Derek's observation of the records, Adam had been squirreling away money and depositing it into his IOLTA account as client's money. Then he transferred it to his father's old savings that he kept on because he had his father's power of attorney and was his executor. Once he started the automatic deposits and transfers then he sat back and accumulated his money before sending it to the Caymans in a manner and way not to trigger reporting requirements. Who changed that after Adam's death?

Sharon had been his executor, but there was no reason for her to allow this set up to continue for four years. She could have closed it out and kept the money. What about Adam's children? Both were adults, and they could have pulled a trick similar to Adam. Kept up a deceased parent's account to get to the money offshore?

No way to know except to talk to them. Not having to return to Atlanta this evening gave him time for their interviews. He locked up the evidence, returned to the B&B to change, and then ate at one of the restaurants surrounding the square. He would catch each child at home after dinner.

Adam Michael Cranford, Jr. who went by the name, Mike, and his wife, Merilee, lived in an older neighborhood a few blocks from the square. Derek found it to be a small house built in the sixties but well maintained and recently modernized. He knocked on the door. Mike answered. Derek showed his credentials and asked if he could talk for a moment.

Mike stood for a moment, concern showing in his face and then he said, "Of course. Merilee and my mother mentioned they met you yesterday."

"Your mother was helpful, but I want to get a rounded picture of your father. The more I know about him, the more I can fit all the pieces together."

Mike led Derek into a homey but messy living room. He said, "Just a minute let me tell my wife you're here. I was on my way to help her give the twins a bath."

At that moment Merliee appeared drying her hands on a towel. "Did I hear the doorbell? Oh, sir, it's you. I didn't realize you were here." She looked at Mike.

He said, "The detective wants to talk to me now. Why don't you go ahead, and I'll catch up in a minute."

She nodded but hesitated.

He leaned over and kissed her on the forehead. "It's O.K. I promise. We won't be long."

She turned and walked up the stairs.

Mike led them to the living room and sat down. "I really can't take too long. Twins are a handful, and I don't want to leave her with all the work."

Derek chose a chair across from Mike that allowed some light from the window to illuminate his face. "That's understandable. I wanted to ask if you were close to your father and had any idea of who would shoot him?"

Mike looked thoughtful. "Close to him? No, I wasn't. I imagine a lot of people wanted to shoot him as he did annoy people sometimes, but I can't imagine anyone actually doing so. I'm afraid I can't be much help."

"So growing up, he didn't take you to ballgames or help with your homework?"

"Oh, I guess sometimes." Mike thought for a moment. "The truth is I didn't see Dad much. He was gone a lot, and I really liked school. I was into lots of activities and some sports. I was just always on the go. I took drama classes and was in plays. Mom took me, and Livvy, to all our clubs, sports, classes etc. Summers my friends were at my house a lot because we had a pool. I just didn't have much free time alone."

"Was your Dad indifferent?"

"Maybe. He was just in the background. He was never mean or cruel like I have friends say about their dads. He didn't drink alcohol, have affairs, or lose his temper. He sort of seemed to play the role assigned to him and that was it."

"So, he never taught you to play chess or sports or taught you to shoot or even warn you about the dangers of life?" Derek smiled slightly.

Mike grimaced. "No, he didn't. I'm not sure I would want him to. I wasn't into chess or shooting, but I did ask him once to help me throw the football when I was about eight. But he said he wasn't very good at that type of thing. I'd better find someone who could help me more."

"You didn't find that an odd statement from a man who was a winning quarterback on his high school team?"

Mike blinked. "They did mention that at his funeral. No, I just thought poor old man. He's really missing out on fun. I asked some guys at school and one of the coaches to help me. I didn't think of it again." He narrowed his eyes, "But now that I do, I realize he could have taught me even if he didn't run anymore. He just didn't want to fool with me."

"Probably he just didn't want to fool with the football. I have the impression it was the strategy in quarterbacking that appealed to him not the sport. I wouldn't take it personally."

"Oh, 'personally'." Mike shrugged. "I learned a long time ago to get on with my life and not stew over what others did. My mother probably taught me that or maybe going to Sunday school."

"Your father did pay for your college tuition, I heard."

"Yes, we never had a lot of extra money, so I was surprised at his offer. But he said he had saved up for it."

"What did you major in?"

"Business. I enjoy that, and Mom's let me take over as CEO of the lumberyard and sawmill. Also, I'm now trustee of her family trust fund."

"I heard your father was not very good at business."

His open and honest expression changed to one of concern. "That's what Mom said. Dad didn't speak about it. I wasn't involved. Too young."

"Didn't you find it odd that he ran his law firm well and had enough for tuition yet failed in other ventures?"

Mike looked down and said, "I didn't give it much thought."

Derek was good at reading faces. Mike was an outgoing man accustomed to being honest and forthright. The effort of trying to cover up was not easy for him. "Didn't you?"

"What, what do you mean?"

"I mean that you obviously are close to your mom, and it's her money that your father lost, or said he did."

Mike looked at Derek and widened his eyes. "What do you mean 'or said he did.'"?

"I mean that his poor business sense and mistakes that resulted in your mother losing money was verbally said, but she didn't ask for an accounting of where it went. It started after your grandfather died. Are you sure the money was 'lost' and not put in your father's pockets?"

Mike winced. "No, I'm not. Mom always said Dad had a poor head for business, so I thought he was just not bright, at least at first."

"When did you think differently and what changed your mind?"

"My second year of college. Studying for my

business major made me look at things differently and start asking questions."

"Did you ask them of your father?"

"I tried to, but he would just play his games."

"Games?"

"Yes, he'd say he didn't know what I was talking about. I must have heard it wrong. By then I knew that was his standard answer to a lot of people in a lot of different situations and realized he wasn't going to answer."

"You didn't force it?"

"No, but I did say I was going to be helping Mom in her businesses now. I'd be glad to advise him on any ventures he wanted to take."

Derek smiled. "Clever and tactful of you. I'm guessing he didn't make any more poor decisions after that."

"No, he didn't."

"Were you aware that he had accounts at State Bank with quite a bit of money amounting to almost $10 million before his death?"

Mike's mouth fell open. "Ten million? Dollars? Where did he get that kind of money and why didn't Mom inherit it?"

"I'm sorry to tell you this, but I think your father was dishonest. He probably took bribes and stole some of your mother's family money. He may have made a lot more money at his law firm than he revealed. After all, he could pay for both yours and your sister's college education without taking out loans."

Mike stared at Derek. "I hope that money is going to Mom?"

"Some of it. I'm afraid most of it disappeared out

of his accounts the day after he died."

"The day after? Who?"

"We don't know. I was hoping you might have learned about those accounts and could help us."

Mike shook his head. "Not a thing. I wasn't an heir. Dad didn't have a will, so it all went to Mom. William helped her with the probate and knows more about it than I ever could, so I didn't see anything about his finances."

"Did you ever help with his computer or anything with his business?"

"No, I can use a computer, but it's not my thing. I'm a people person. I like dealing with sales targets and employees and other challenges. Dad was the opposite. He kept everything to himself and never asked anyone for help."

Derek nodded. Either Mike gained very good acting skills at those drama lessons, or the accounts were a genuine surprise to him.

The sound of water splashing came from upstairs and a child giggling. Mike looked up. His thoughts seemed to quickly move from his dad to his family. "I need to help my wife. If you need to speak some more, could we set a time for tomorrow?"

"No need. I appreciate your help."

Derek left with the impression Mike may have the same name but a very different character and personality than his father. And that he was not the person who accessed the accounts after his father's death.

Chapter 11:
The Daughter

Elizabeth, nicknamed "Livvy," was the daughter and lived several miles out in the country with her husband. Since daylight lingered late this time of year, Derek wanted to fit the visit in before dark. The couple did not have children so perhaps they would be free at this time.

In response to his knock a woman in her twenties, a little overweight, but active looking came to the door. He could see the resemblance to her mother, but she had inherited her short height from her father. He showed her his credentials and introduced himself as he had done with the others.

She smiled, "Sure, Mom told me about you. My husband is here, and he'll join us if you don't mind."

"Not at all. I'm trying to understand more about your father since I never met him."

Derek stepped into a farmhouse built about ten years ago, unlike the older homes favored by the mother and brother.

Elizabeth said, "Actually I can't help with that much. I didn't really know my father very well. Would you like a glass of tea?"

"No thanks, I just ate."

A large muscular man in his twenties wearing farm overalls walked into the room from the back. "I saw a car drive up. Oh, hello."

"Hon, this is the cold case detective that's investigating Dad's murder."

"I'm Derek Fielding, and your name is?"

"Rick. Nice to meet you," he said and offered his hand.

Manners out of the way, Derek followed the couple to a den with a large gas fireplace and comfortable easy chairs and sofas scattered around. A large TV screen was attached over the mantle.

"I'm sorry to come so late, but I have limited time and won't keep you long."

Elizabeth had long light brown hair pulled back in a ponytail with an elastic band, "Oh, that's fine. We were just finishing for the day. We're farmers. At least we're starting to farm, and we just finished our chores. What did you want to know? As I said, I didn't know much about Dad's work."

"Did he ever talk about his money or plans or business ventures with you?"

"Not that I remember. In fact, I didn't notice it at the time, but we didn't talk about much at all."

By now Derek understood the family dynamics, but asked, "Can you be more specific?"

She looked at her husband and shrugged. "He wasn't around much and like my brother, I really liked school. I did a lot of things. I was in the drama group, played soccer, tried out for cheerleading, and the computer club. I was always going and doing stuff. Mom took me to most things. We did some outings as a family, but we never talked about our feelings. I guess we did with Mom but not Dad."

"Not even to play chess or go shooting or hunting?"

Elizabeth laughed. "Never. I don't think Dad did any of those things, and I sure didn't. In high school I discovered I really liked computers and joined the computer club. That's what my degree is in: computer science. I've started my own web design company. I can do that at home and still help Rick with the farm." She smiled at her husband.

Derek looked at Rick, "Did you also know Mr. Cranford?"

"No, we never met. Livvy and I met in college, and he was deceased by then."

Derek turned back to Elizabeth. "Were you here that 4th of July? I didn't see that mentioned in my notes?"

"No, I was gone. I graduated in May and then left for college early to attend a computer summer camp. I was away when Dad was shot. I came back for the funeral, but I had to go back pretty quickly."

"So, you know a lot about computers?"

Livvy nodded her ponytail flopping up and down. "Yes, more than I want to. I can fix computers, install software, and do security, but I prefer just to do web design."

"Did your father ask you to work on his computer?"

"No, Dad never really asked people to do things for him, and I doubt he would have much confidence in my skills anyway."

"Did you resent him or wish he paid you more attention?"

Elizabeth looked astonished. "No, why would I want that?"

"Most children like their parent's attention and praise."

"Mom praised me. Dad, well, he was never mean or abusive to me like I've heard one of my friends complain about her parents. He never yelled or shouted or showed anger. I didn't have any reason to resent him. I guess Mom gave me everything I needed, emotionally, and church did also. I'm a Christian and have a fellowship with other believers. Dad just wasn't important. I guess that's terrible to say."

"Not at all. He wasn't a big part of your life, which sounds quite full."

"It was. In fact, a lot of my friends were usually around at the house. We had the only in-ground swimming pool for my age group. We often stayed at my house during the summer. I sure didn't feel neglected by my dad. I would have felt awkward if he had joined us."

Derek did not think his next question would gain much information but was surprised. "Did you know your father had separate bank accounts at State Bank?"

"Yes, I figured he did. Or at least he did some business there. I saw him coming out of the bank there a couple of times when I was on the cheerleader squad, and we had day games in that town."

"Did you tell your mother or brother?"

"I don't think so. It wouldn't occur to me. It was just Dad doing business. He was often around the county being a commissioner and having law clients."

"Did you see him at any other banks?"

Elizabeth looked down at the floor and thought.

"Not that I remember. That stood out in my mind because he had a checkbook or something in his hand. I'm not into business like Mike, but I'm detailed and notice things like that. Also, when I was older one of my friends worked there my last year of high school. I met her for lunch and remembered having seen Dad there. "

"Did you help your mother with probate or your father's finances?"

Elizabeth shook her head. "That was my first year of college. Mom and William handled everything. I've been gone for four years. I just finished this past May. Rick and I've been married about a year now, so we've been really busy."

"I can understand. Speaking of computers, did you ever hear your mother or anyone mention your father's laptop?"

Elizabeth narrowed her eyes and thought for a moment. "I don't recall it. I guess it stayed with the business."

"No, it was picked up by the police forensic techs after your father's death, but I discovered when I turned it on this week that it has been completely wiped clean of software and data, including any and all files. Did your father have the kind of skills to set that up?"

Elizabeth stared at him. "Really? All of it? That's strange. I don't think Dad did or more importantly, I can't imagine why he would. I remember his talking about how client records are really important, and he had to keep them safe."

"Do you know if he did backups of his computer?"

"I remember when I was young, he did CD disks and then went to flash drives because he asked me how to find the right one when they first came out."

"What did you tell him?"

"I explained they fit into a USB slot, and that they had different amount of storage in Gigs, usually."

"Do you know if he used them?"

"I assume so."

"Any idea where he kept them?"

"Not at work, but he did have an office at home. I think he had a metal box he locked stuff in on the bookshelf. Kind of a brown metal thing."

"That's helpful."

"Sure, I don't know why Dad would erase everything on his computer. I mean he carried it around with him most places. I'm sure he had it with him before I left for college."

"When was that?"

"I guess at my graduation day. He carried it home the night before, and we all attended the ceremony the next day. He didn't work. We went to a reception, and he talked to a lot of people about his county commissioner job. Then we came home, and I remember seeing him leave with it the next morning."

"Do you know what kind he had or his password?"

"Yes, it was a Windows PC, but I never saw the password. Like I said he never asked me to do anything for him, but we did talk about which brand of computer was better and printers and stuff. But I felt like he asked me more as a technical expert than a daughter because I was in a computer club, and we did a lot with new technologies."

"Understood. Sounds like you were very knowledgeable, even before your degree."

"Just the usual things that you learn with high

school geeks. Mainly we tried to design programs and new apps, but they didn't always work. Sometimes we did things we shouldn't such as explore the dark web or try to hack the school's computers. Fortunately, they had a good system we couldn't breach, and no one got in trouble for trying."

"Do you think your father could have accidently set up his computer to erase itself?"

"Dad was very clever, but I don't see him being careless. I don't know of a way to do that accidentally, but I guess it could happen. Honestly, it sounds more like a malware attack, like the ones where your data is held to ransom unless you pay the hackers. But even that would have some sort of message on it. Did you see a big bold text message?"

"I can't comment on that."

"I see, well, sorry, I can't help with that. I think you'd have to ask Tammy at the office. She would have seen him use it more than me."

"Thanks, I appreciate your help."

Rick had not said much but now he asked, "Do you think it's possible to find out who shot him after all these years? I mean it's been kind of hard for Livvy and her family putting up with whispers that I've noticed since we moved here. It would be nice to get it solved and the person arrested."

Derek said, "I agree, and I'm working on it."

Rick said, "We're praying that you're successful."

"Yes, we are," nodded Elizabeth.

Derek smiled. "I appreciate that. Have a nice evening."

When he stepped outside, the gentle summer evening had descended. As he walked to his car, he listened to crickets and mosquitos and a few frogs from a nearby pond. What he'd really like to hear was a beep of a text from Megan. Where was she this evening?

Turning his mind back to his last interview, he felt less certain about the daughter's innocence than the son's. She knew about State Bank and had access to his computer. She said they didn't talk, but they had about technical aspects of computers. She seemed open and unconcerned, but she had also taken computer classes and studied acting.

Derek returned to his B&B suite and started to write up his notes when Megan texted. She had been tied up due to a delayed vote and the legislature was meeting again in the morning. She was waiting to talk to the head of a nonprofit fighting the bill and would be really late tonight on his time zone. She would call in the morning and sent her love.

He grinned. Megan was engrossed in a hot story and having fun pursuing it. He could read between the text lines. At least she was OK. No gangsters after her, which had happened.

Chapter 12:
Another Suspect

Derek decided to track down the flash drive early the next morning. It would be a long shot, but he suspected not much had changed in Sharon's house since the murder. She had a new husband and grandchildren but not new furniture.

When he knocked on the front door, William came to open it with a cup of coffee in one hand and dressed for work. "Detective Fielding. We were just about to leave. Can I help you?"

"I wanted to speak to Sharon for a quick moment. It won't be long."

Sharon came around the corner, also ready for her day. "How can I help?"

"I spoke to Elizabeth last night, and she tells me that Adam kept a backup of his computer info on a flash drive in a brown metal box on your bookshelf. I know it's a long shot, but do you still have that?"

Sharon blinked at him. "I may. Adam worked at our library desk, and I remember going through his papers but not finding a flash drive. I do know the box. Why don't we look?"

William opened the door wider for him to step in. Derek stepped into the cool entranceway and followed them down the wood hallway to a room lined with bookshelves. Some shelves had books. Others had knickknacks and photos.

She said, "We used to use this room for Livvy and Mike's study groups, but now it's seldom used unless William needs the desk. I think there was a metal box on that shelf at one time, but it has stuffed animal toys there now."

William said, "Didn't you childproof the house when the twins started to visit? I remember you talking about the need."

"Oh, yes, I did!" exclaimed Sharon. She raised her eyes to a higher shelf. "I moved everything that was easily reachable and breakable up to a higher level."

William walked over to a top shelf and ran his hand along it. "I feel metal. Is this it?" He pulled a metal box in front of a picture frame and lifted it down. "Shall I open it?"

"Please do," she said.

William turned the key left in the lock and lifted the lid. A flash drive was nestled on a folded computer screen dust cloth. Derek tried not to catch his breath.

William smiled. "I supposed you want us to just give you this with a receipt?"

Derek smiled back, "Yes, sir. It would save time not to have to get a warrant and for me to wait here while someone in the Sheriff's office brings it. That way I can confirm it wasn't switched while I went to get it."

William looked at Sharon. "It's yours, dear."

"Give it to him, by all means. I'll get some paper for a receipt."

While Sharon pulled a tablet out of a drawer,

William said, "I'm surprised you're looking for this. Surely the techs got everything off his computer four years ago."

"There was nothing on his computer."

"Nothing? You mean of use?"

"That too. His computer was wiped, not only of data, but every software program."

William raised his eyebrows. "But he had to have the legal software we use for searching cases and laws. We certainly pay a lot for it every month. Also, his client accounts and court documents would need to be on it."

"He may have, but it was wiped clean a few hours after the shooting."

William stared. "After the shooting? Someone did that to his computer? Why? I don't think mine or Tammy's was touched. And I don't remember anything stolen."

"We don't know. One of the mysteries that have come to light now."

Sharon handed him a handwritten receipt which he signed. Her face lit up. "You have information leading to a new suspect?"

"We have information that shows someone had computer knowledge."

Her face clouded again, "Livvy does, but surely you aren't thinking of her? She wasn't in town and was only just out of high school."

Derek folded the paper and pulled a plastic evidence bag out of his jacket pocket and tilted the can sideways to drop the drive in without touching it. "We are still asking questions to gather information. I can't comment. I can say that Sheriff Tagger is willing to hire a private computer firm that does disk recovery to see what we can find."

William frowned. "This is getting more complicated than a simple shooting."

Derek said, "I agree. Thanks for your help." He left them standing and staring after him as he drove back to his office. He had a lot to do today.

As he walked down the hall and past Tagger's open door, he looked in and nodded. Tagger said, "Hi Fielding. I have some news for you."

Derek stopped and backed up to walk into the office, "I hope it's good news."

"I think so. Have a seat, and I'll go over it. Or do you want to put your stuff in your office first?"

"I'd prefer to hear what you got."

"We got fingerprints off those guns in Adam's safe deposit box. One gun has the prints of a man suspected of shooting his wife's lover, but he's since died. The second has the prints of a woman who was charged with shooting her boyfriend while both were on drugs at a local hotel. She claimed he attacked her, and he claimed she tried to kill him to steal his drugs. The charges were dropped since there was no proof either way and no gun. Also, the boyfriend had a superficial wound. We're looking for the woman who lives near Savannah off one of those private barrier islands. But the statute of limitations has run on it, so no charges could be filed now. That leaves no real motive to pay blackmail or shoot Adam that we can see.

"The other gun is a different story. It has to do with the other cold case I was going to ask you to look into. If we're right on the ballistics test, you won't need to. So far, we've only had time to test for fingerprints. They show clearly in the spots where you would hold a gun to shoot it and are not smudged. They match one of Adam's clients from about ten years ago. His name is Samuel Vickers. His wife was killed by a single gunshot to the head and not found for a couple of weeks until her sister decided to go check on her. Samuel is a long-distance truck driver and said he was out of town during that time. The records show he had a load that day but not when he left his home. He had a gun registered to him that matched the type of gun and bullet caliber. When we asked to test it, he said that someone stole it from him on a road trip. Samuel was brought in and questioned several times, but Adam Cranford was his attorney and very aggressive in representing him. Sam and his wife had frequent fights and both drank. The case went nowhere without other suspects. I was working in the department then, but I was on traffic and wasn't involved in homicide. This is the gun Sam says was stolen. There are no other prints on it, including Adam's. We will need to send it to ballistics for confirmation, but my guess is that Adam offered to keep it or took it somehow and has been blackmailing Samuel ever since."

Derek said, "That would explain the plastic bag used to preserve it."

Tagger nodded. "That might explain the cash deposits in the IOLTA account and the safety deposit box. I also rechecked the case notes to see if we lifted any fingerprints on the wad of money in Adam's hand when he was shot. Unfortunately, it was soaked in blood and none recoverable. It would be nice to find Samuel's prints on the money."

Derek frowned, "I see the similar MO and motive,

but is Samuel Vickers rich? Those are a lot of deposits for one blackmail victim. I wonder if blackmail was another side business for Adam with many of his clients."

"I wouldn't be surprised."

Derek said, "It opens up the field for more suspects. And it could account for the computer being erased if incriminating documents were kept on it."

Tagger smiled. "We might close two cold cases at once if Samuel shot Adam."

Derek looked thoughtful. "The only problem is that if Samuel shot Adam, why didn't he get access to the gun? Why not force Adam to give it to him?"

"Good questions. He still drives a rig but not as much and is thinking of retirement last I heard. Maybe he just had enough and shot Adam and hoped the gun was lost in probate. Rather hard to pay blackmail on a retirement income."

"Are you going to seek an arrest warrant without the ballistics report?"

"Yes, I've asked for one and got it. I know he's in town this week, so we're going to bring him in for questioning and arrest him, if necessary. One reason I've mentioned it is to ask if you want to sit in on his interview?"

"Yes, I would. Are you going out yourself or asking an officer to bring him in?"

"Myself and another officer. I wanted to observe his reaction. Do you want to go?"

"Yes, if you have time to let me get back to my office and get situated."

Tagger glanced up at the clock. "What about 15 minutes? You can also catch me up on Adam's case as we drive. I understand you interviewed the children last night?"

Derek laughed. "Small town gossip or complaints?"

"Small town chat at the morning diner. You would be surprised what I hear."

"I'm sure I would. But before I leave with you, I have another item that needs to be checked for prints. I want to take it with me when I carry the computer to Lisa's company. The daughter told me Adam had a flash drive from his computer stored at home, and Sharon found one, hopefully, the same one in the box the daughter described he kept it in."

Tagger raised his eyebrows. "Amazing. If you have the evidence bag, I can have them check it while we go out to Sam's house."

Derek agreed.

As they were driving, Tagger asked, "Other than the flash drive do you have anything else new?"

Derek said, "A better understanding of possible family motivation from talking to the children. Mike discovered his father was stealing from his mother and not a poor businessman as thought when he was in college. He tried to confront Adam who pretended ignorance, but there were no more poor business decisions after that. Also, the daughter was in the high school computer club before going on to get a computer science degree. Neither seems to hold a grudge or have any strong feelings towards their father, but then they both studied acting."

"So, the son might have had the motivation and the daughter the skills to wipe the computer?"

"Yes, but if the stealing stopped and the daughter

was starting her college degree, I see no motivation at all. Also, both seem very well adjusted. Shooting your father in cold blood takes a very dysfunctional mindset."

Tagger shook his head. "I'm sure you're like me and have seen people do things you would not have thought them capable of, but I agree that's not likely with those two. In fact, I can't imagine any of the suspect's we've had up to now shoot Adam. Sharon and William are sincere Christians, Freda merely an aggressive saleswoman, and the two children did not profit by his death much less have the mindset. However, I can see Sam shooting Adam if he was fed up with blackmail and had a drink or two to celebrate the 4th."

Derek nodded. He did not have the same confidence in Sam. "Would Sam have stopped to erase the computer or would he have had the skills for the single shot dead center, especially if he was drunk?"

"Good questions. But, if not Sam, where does that leave us? Another blackmail victim?"

"What the French call *Personne Inconnue*, the unknown person. Someone we've yet to find."

Tagger growled, "Let's leave the French out of this. We've got too many people in this mess already."

Derek laughed. "Gladly."

They soon turned into a dirt road that stopped at a house built several decades ago but not maintained. The grass needed mowing, and a fence leading to a barn was in need of repair. A garage also need paint and several shingles were missing from its roof. However, a clean and new looking long-haul truck stood in the driveway. Perhaps after four years of no blackmail payments, Sam had more money to buy a truck.

The Sheriff stopped in front, and his deputy took the back. The Sheriff knocked and shouted, "Police," but Sam did not answer. The Sheriff knocked again and repeated his demand for Sam to come to the door. Silence was the only response.

Sheriff Tagger spoke into his phone, "Bill, we're getting no response. Do you hear any sounds from inside from your location?"

"Negative, Sheriff."

Sheriff Tagger raised his arm, knocked and repeated himself. "I suppose he could be gone, but....."

After the last knock the door slowly opened wide making a slight creaking sound. Sheriff Tagger and Derek both held their guns ready. Still no sound only silence.

"At this point, I think we're justified in going in on a wellness check, if nothing else. Why is his truck outside, the door unlocked or latched, and no one answering?" asked Tagger.

"After you," said Derek and promptly followed him in, both men ready for attack.

They finally heard a noise. It was the sound of snoring. Sam lay on his back on the sofa gently snoring. Apparently, he was a very sound sleeper.

Sheriff Tagger shook him by the shoulder and said, "Wake up, Sam. What's wrong with you? Didn't you hear me knocking?"

Sam looked at the Sheriff and blinked. "Hey Sheriff, whatcha want? I've been driving straight for two days. Now's not a good time to visit."

"I have a warrant for your arrest. I want to bring you in for questioning."

Sam shook his head and struggled to sit up. He yawned. "Huh! We've been through this before. You don't have evidence to arrest me."

"We've dragged up a gun with your fingerprints on it that Adam Cranford had in his safe deposit box."

"Well, I guess I need to find another lawyer then."

Tagger read Sam his rights, cuffed him, and then the accompanying officer drove Sam back to the police department. Derek and Tagger followed. Derek was glad he came for the arrest and saw Sam's reaction. The man had answered without concern when first seeing the Sheriff. Derek suspected that Sam, like everyone in this county, knew Adam's case was being re-investigated. Was his unconcern real or fake?

Chapter 13:
Samuel Mark Vickers

Derek looked at his cell phone. Noon and no call from Megan since an earlier text saying she might need to stay until tomorrow. He wondered if he could still make it to Lisa's office today. Especially since the fingerprint crew had not yet returned the flash drive, and Sam could not find an attorney until after lunch. He would push his trip to Atlanta back until tomorrow, unless Megan came back in tonight.

Derek used the time after Sam's arrest to read the case notes on the wife's death. No other fingerprints in the house, door left unlocked but nothing stolen, the wife stayed home most of the time and was a known alcoholic. She had been in and out of jail for disorderly conduct and was known to become violent under the influence. Derek wondered if Adam had taken advantage of Sam for his own purposes. An honest lawyer might have pled for self-defense. The D.A. might have chosen not to prosecute. Sam might have lived a life free of jail and no blackmail. No way to know now.

Derek called Lisa and explained the delay. She agreed and said since tomorrow was only Thursday, they would still have time to work on it. If necessary, she was willing to work on Friday, even though it was a company holiday. Derek thanked her and turned back to his notes.

It would be interesting to match Sam's withdrawals with Adam's deposits if he could get them. Derek looked up as an officer knocked on his door and told him that the Sheriff was starting the interview now.

Derek entered the room to find the Sheriff sitting at a table facing Sam and a young woman wearing a white blouse and a black suit with a tablet in front of her. Tagger introduced her as the public defender, Ms. Julie Randolph.

Derek acknowledged the introduction. Tagger went through the preliminaries and said, "OK, Mr. Vickers, you've had time to talk with your attorney, and we would like your cooperation in answering our questions."

Ms. Randolph said, "I have explained to Mr. Vickers that he has the right to remain silent."

Taggers nodded but didn't look at her. "Sam, it's been ten years since your wife was shot. At that time, you told us your gun was stolen with the serial number we've provided to you and your attorney. Yet, we found it in Adam Cranford's safety deposit box in a plastic bag with only your figure prints on it and no one else's, including Adam's. Why did you tell us it was stolen when Adam had it?"

"Well, uh, uh, I don't know."

Derek noticed that Tagger did not ask about the interaction between Adam and Sam as their interaction was protected with confidentiality laws."

"The fact that you lied shows obstruction of a police investigation, and your fingerprints show you were the last person to have it."

"Uh, well, uh..."

Ms. Randolph said, "The ballistic tests have not yet proven that is the gun that shot Mrs. Vickers."

Tagger looked at Sam, "Sam, you know what they will show. You know if that test will let you walk free or convict you of your wife's murder."

Sam looked down at the table and blinked, "Yeah....I know. That scum Cranford...," he stopped.

"Tell us what happened. I know Darlene could be violent at times. Adam never let us find out what happened. So, we never had the chance to find out if it was self-defense. The D.A. might not have prosecuted if you had convinced him of that."

Ms. Randolph said, "That's speculation."

Sam sighed, "I'm so tired of all this and that scum Adam took me for so much money. Yeah, the tests will show it's my gun, but it was an accident. Darlene was drinking, but I wasn't. I had to leave to pick up a load and didn't want to get a DUI. She kept yelling that I was worthless and leaving her all the time. But she had her own money, plenty of food in the house, and her own car. Her family lived nearby. She wasn't helpless. When I packed my bag and got my keys, Darlene started screaming at me and stood in front of the door. When I tried to walk past her, she shoved me, and I fell backwards. I dropped my overnight bag. I grabbed to put back my stuff. The gun was in it, and Darlene shoved me again just as I grabbed it, and it went off. I thought the safety was on, but I guess not. I didn't use it much. I just kept it for protection. The bullet went through her head, and she was gone instantly. I couldn't believe it. I called Adam since I knew him. He told me to put the gun in a plastic bag and come see him. I'd write him a check as a retainer, and he'd represent me. I told him I couldn't leave Darlene like that, but he said I couldn't help her, and I needed to save myself. I needed the money from my job and did what he said. He took the gun and said that an attorney couldn't reveal what a client said."

Tagger said, "Tell me about Adam's blackmail payments."

"What is there to tell? He fought to keep them from arresting me and then started saying I had to make storage payments for the gun. I figured out pretty quick that it was extortion but not much I could do. I paid for six years and then, thankfully, someone shot him, and I was free of those payments. I waited for someone to ask about the gun, but no one did. I decided they threw it away or something."

"How did you make your payments?"

"What do you mean?"

"In cash, ACH, check? When and how much?"

"Oh, always in cash. Once every six months. Adam demanded a thousand dollars in cash. I would go to my savings and take it out. It hurt financially, but I could live without it, and it was better than being in jail."

"When was the last payment you made?"

Sam looked at the attorney. "Is this part of Darlene's case? I don't have to answer otherwise, do I?"

Tagger said before the attorney responded, "We're asking you as a helpful witness to our investigation for Adam's killer. We're not charging you with it. Also, cooperating would help the D.A. look kindly on your wife's case, perhaps."

The attorney said, "We would need to talk to him

about that. If that's all..."

Derek spoke up, "Can you tell us how you paid the thousand dollars? Was it all in an envelope? Tied up in packages?"

Sam looked at him. "Does it matter?"

Derek nodded.

"The bank put those paper things around it, and there was $250.00 in each one for a total of four."

Tagger said, "Adam had one just like that in his hand when he was shot. He had $250.00 tied in a paper wrapper."

Sam stared at him. "Look if you're accusing me of shooting Adam, think again. If I were to shoot him, I'd take my money back. In fact, I wouldn't give it to him in the first place. Also, why would I shoot him? He had the gun used against my wife." Tagger said, "I heard you were planning to retire. It might be harder to pay blackmail on a retirement income."

"I get a nice retirement from my company when I do retire, and a thousand dollars each six months wouldn't break me. But I am tired of people looking at me and wondering. They don't do it as much now but still...I met this nice lady, and she lives in Tennessee. I've been thinking about selling up and moving there with her. We'd get married, but she's a Christian and says I need to make everything right with the Lord. I didn't kill Adam, but I would like to confess about Darlene. If I'm in jail, maybe my Tennessee lady will still love me and visit."

Derek said, "That's a strong motivation. I've been a homicide detective for ten years. Your story is not uncommon where alcohol is involved and an abusive spouse. But you can help your case a lot by telling us more about Adam. We suspect you were not the only client he had, but we think you were the one there the night he died. Knowing more about that night will help us find the real killer."

Sam closed his eyes, "Oh man, oh man, this is so unreal. I did not shoot Adam. But I was there that night. I arrived right after the fireworks started. I guess that was about 10:00."
"He was waiting on your payment? That's why he was in his office late on July 4th?"

"Yes, I didn't get to town often and with all the people for the concert, it was easy to meet him then. He sent me an email saying the time and place as he usually did. He seemed the same as usual. Sneering at me and taking my money. In fact, I have no way to prove it, but he told me that was the last payment. So that would give me even less reason to kill him."

"You gave him four wrapped sections of $250.00 each?" asked Derek.

"Yes, wasn't it there?"

"No."

Sam's eyes widened. "That's odd."

"Tell us why it was the last payment."

"He said he was leaving town for good. I asked for my gun back. He just laughed and said he might mail it to me. There was nothing I could do, so I called him some names and threw down the money on the desk and left."

"Was anyone else in the office?"

"Not that I saw or heard. There was a lot of noise outside with the concert and then the fireworks going off."

"What about his computer? Where was it?"

"Computer? I have no idea."

"Can you think back? Was it on his desk, open or closed?"

Sam closed his eyes. "I think he had a laptop sitting on a side desk or small conference table that he turned sideways to and could work. It wasn't on his desk where I put the bills."

"Did you see a brown wooden decorative box on his desk?"

Sam again closed his eyes and thought. "Yes, I think there was something. It sat right on the edge towards the door. I tossed the bills over it towards him. I couldn't see what was in it. It was closed."

Derek asked, "One more question, do you know if the laptop was turned on? For example, did you see a screen saver or data on it?"

Sam thought again. "I just don't remember. I was focused on that creep. He really enjoyed jerking someone around. I'm not surprised someone shot him, but it wasn't me. Besides I've never bought another gun. After Darlene, I had a horror of the things. I'm not even a good shot. If I was going to kill Adam, I would have strangled him or punched him in the head. I'm a lot bigger and stronger, especially four years ago, and he was out of shape."

Derek was not surprised by that statement. He asked one more question, "Did you see anyone approaching the office when you left?"

Sam shook his head. "I was so mad. I really didn't pay attention. There were a lot of people around, though most were looking at the fireworks."

"Most but not all?"

"A man and woman were leaving. She was carrying a little dog that was trembling and she was talking to it like it was a baby. I wondered why would she bring an animal to fireworks? Most don't like the explosions."

"Anyone else?"

"No...oh, yeah there was one of the performers."
"A singer?"

"Maybe, she had on an Uncle Sam costume and was walking behind the couple so I couldn't see her very well."

"But you're sure she was a woman?"

"Yeah, she seemed to have the right curves."

"Tall or short."

"About average I guess."

"Anyone else?"

"Now that I'm thinking about that night, I do remember hearing a truck or some vehicle other than a car at the corner of the building and wondering who was driving past the barriers."

Derek said, "Thanks for your help. I don't have any more questions, but if you can get a copy of that email it would help."

"I still have that account, so I'll look back for it. It was a special account Adam used, not the business one."

Derek widened his eyes, "What was the name on that account?"

"I think it was like travel days at one of those free accounts like gmail or yahoo."

Tagger said, "Your hearing is tomorrow. If the judge allows it, do you have anyone to help you to make bail?"

"I think my friend, her name is Maybelle, will help, but I'm not sure yet."

Tagger ended the interview and an officer led Sam away with the attorney following behind. Tagger and Derek walked back to Tagger's office.

Tagger sat down in his chair, leaned back, and said, "What are your thoughts on this? Do you think he shot Adam?"

"No. I don't."

"Why?"

"For the reasons he named, particularly about the money. He would not have left part of it in Adam's hands or given it to him in the first place. He would have shown up, shot him and left. Why give him cash?"

Tagger nodded. "I agree. But who?"

"I think it's significant that Adam was planning on leaving. That matches the airline ticket copy."

"So you think Adam was taking a trip to the Caymans and not coming back?"

"I do. Adam's life was closing down around him. Freda was demanding the entire county sign a petition asking for an investigation of his finances. Sharon would ask for an accounting if she got a legal separation or divorce. Adam's dream was to travel. He gave it up after his marriage, and his father-in-law kept him from stealing while he was alive. Sharon said Adam was a planner and good at strategy. That's why he was a good quarterback. I think Adam lived for his dream and drifted along in life not really touched by anything or anyone. He schemed and planned for his life of travel one day. He siphoned off profits from his business, took bribes and used blackmail, but it caught up with him. I think he was greedy and waited for

Sam's last payment before he left without a word to anyone."

"So, what went wrong?"

"I don't know," said Derek. "The most likely is another blackmail victim, but it would need to be someone who knew him well enough to know about the accounts and had access to his computer."

"That sounds more like a coworker or family member. Are we back to them?"

"I don't think we ever left them. We've just widened our circle. But I do finally know when and where to find Mayor Andrew and Sharon's sister. Freda is right. He's good at avoiding people."

Chapter 14:
The Mayor and the Sister

Derek caught Mayor Andrew Harris and Cece Vincent Harris at home. After voicemails not returned, referrals to assistants who weren't in their office, and other detours of misdirection; he had finally found an employee who said the mayor had a planning meeting at the library today. However, the mayor had left to eat lunch at home first.

Derek felt no guilt in interrupting the lunch. The mayor knew he was looking for him. In fact he seemed resigned, but not surprised, when his wife answered the door and led Derek into their dining room.

Derek showed him his credentials and then said, "As you know, I'm investigating the cold case of Adam Cranford's homicide four years ago. I understand you and your wife went to the 4th of July fireworks concert that night?" Derek had decided to start with an easy question, at least he thought it was.

"Well," Andrew glanced at his wife. "Well, yes, we did go to the fireworks concert."

Cece said, "Yes, such a patriotic thing to do each year."

Derek looked at her.

"Yes, as Mayor, I generally give a little speech to open the concert."

Derek could see the mayor's evasive style continued in person.

"I understand you and Adam did not get along, Mayor?"

Andrew looked startled. "Who told you that? I never argued with Adam."

"I heard you didn't like him?"

"Oh, 'like'! He was my brother-in-law. He wasn't a friend."

"What about politics?"

"Adam was a county commissioner and I'm mayor of the town, so we didn't interact much in our roles."

"What about the development of the downtown? I heard you and Adam both supported maintaining its current historic preservation."

"That's true. What does that have to do with his death?"

Derek wondered also. "I'm trying to get a clear picture of Adam and his interactions with his family and business associates, including the political realm."

"Then you need to speak to his family, his partner, or his clients. I had little to do with Adam except at family reunions and as a property owner in our town where his office building is. Of course, now Sharon owns that, and I think she's put William's name on the deed also."

Cece said, "William is such a nice man. I always thought my sister chose poorly with Adam."

Derek asked, "Did your sister bring an overnight bag and come to stay with you the afternoon of the 4th?"

Cece responded, "Yes, we have a guestroom, and I told her she could stay as long as needed."

"What time did you all leave for the concert?"

Andrew looked at Cece, "Was it about 8 p.m.? The concert started at 9 p.m. and I needed to speak to our city manager about a few things."

"Yes, about 8."

"Was Sharon here when you left?"

"Yes," said Cece.

"What time did you return?"

Andrew stared at Derek. "Return?"

"Yes, from the concert. What time did you get home?"

Andrew looked at Cece again. "About 12 p.m or 1 a.m.?"

Cece nodded. "Yes."

"Which? 12 p.m. or 1 a.m.?" asked Derek, wondering why asking these two people such simple questions was like pulling teeth.

Cece looked at Andrew, "I think 12 p.m.."

"Was Sharon here when you returned?"

Cece said, "I don't know. I didn't look in her room."

Andrew said, "When we left, she was very weepy and looked fatigued. I can't imagine her leaving."

Derek refrained from sighing. "So where were you between 10:00 p.m. and 11:00 p.m then?"

Cece looked at Andrew who looked at Derek. "Why do you ask?"

"Can you just answer the question?"

"You don't think either of us killed Adam, do you?"

"I don't know. Did you?"

"Of course not," exclaimed Cece.

Derek looked at Andrew who said, "No, neither of us were anywhere near his office then."

"Where were you then?"

Silence.

"No one saw you at the concert after your speech."

Cece said, "Maybe he won't tell anyone else, Andrew."

"We don't know that, Cece. This is a murder investigation."

"If it's not relevant to my investigation, then I have no reason to share my knowledge with the public or in court. Where were you both after the mayor made his speech?"

Cece said, "The truth is that Andrew doesn't like crowds of people and loud music, so we went to a little restaurant in Atlanta we both like. No one from Lahillsville goes there. We can get a nice glass of wine and listen to music without someone interrupting us and asking questions."

"Like one of the townspeople," said Andrew as if Derek needed the clarification.

Ah, a mayor who didn't like to meet the people who voted for him. An impediment for a small-town politician, for sure. "If you will give me the name of the restaurant, I will try to find some way to prove your alibi."

"That shouldn't be a problem," said Cece. "We go there every 4th of July and on other holidays too. We know the owner. Andrew went to college with him."

Derek left with the name of the friend who may or may not lie for an old college chum. However, there should be credit card receipts and other hard evidence still available. Of course, their story left Sharon without an alibi.

Chapter 15:
A Very Lively Corpse

Derek got into his SUV and looked at his phone. No calls, emails, or texts. He returned to his office in thought. The evasive maneuvers of Andrew and Cece Harris seemed to be more a way of life and dislike of his constituents than evidence of guilt, unless they were helping Sharon. He said as much to Sheriff Tagger when he found him in his office.

Tagger said, "That sounds like Andrew. He's very good at avoiding those trusting people who vote for him. Leaves a good impression but doesn't do much."

"I'll contact the restaurant and see what his friend says and if any waiters or waitresses have been there over four years."

"Yes, part of the trouble is going back so far." Derek agreed. "I wish we could find the actual airline ticket, but I guess it was thrown out. The photocopy only contains part of it. I wonder if it was purchased as a single or one of a pair. Maybe he was going with someone else. I think I'll call the airlines and see if I can get a copy of the whole purchase package."

"Would they have that information after this long? Warrants given to airlines are often bogged down with red tape and elusive supervisors, as I'm sure you know."

Derek nodded, "I just want to ask some general questions. I'll try that first."

He walked back to his office. Sitting down in his chair, he leaned back and called the airlines to ask how he could get a copy of a ticket when he only had a partial photocopy of it. He gave the information he had and waited. Eventually a professional voice said, "There was only one ticket you purchased. Didn't you keep your receipt after using it?"

"What?"

"That ticket was used on July 10th of that year by Mr. Adam Cranford. Are you Mr. Cranford?"

Derek was not easily surprised, but he was stunned to silence.

"Sir, are you there?"

"Yes. Are you sure it was used?"

"Yes. From Atlanta to the Cayman Islands as purchased in the name of Mr. Adam Cranford. If you're Mr. Cranford, you should have a copy of your portion."

"Thanks. That's fine."

Derek disconnected the call. He gazed at the ceiling and closed his eyes. They would need to get a warrant for that information after all. He doubted any CCTV film would be available this far out. But who erased Adam's computer, transferred his money, and then left for the Cayman Islands?

At that moment, Megan called. Derek looked at the phone, smiled and said, "Hi, Darling. Have you been having fun?"

Megan laughed. "Fun is not the right word. I've been tied up with this crazy story and sitting in legislatures that move as fast as molasses where I couldn't take my phone. Then I got stuck in a building with a bunch of protestors and didn't have my phone there either. I was afraid you would forget me." "Not likely. You're very memorable. I was getting a little concerned, but I knew you were likely busy. Is this a good story?"

"Very." Megan went into detail with her problems tracking down politicians and nonprofit advocates.

Derek enjoyed hearing her voice. He asked, "Are you still coming in tonight? I can drive down after work."

"I have to get this story written, and it would be the middle of the night your time before I arrive. I'd rather get this finished first and fly in tomorrow morning. Would that give you more time to use on the case? Or have you solved it yet?"

"No, I have a very lively corpse who took a plane to the Cayman Islands six days after he was shot and killed."

"Well, I hope he's not on my plane."

"Unlikely, he also carried off ten million dollars to enjoy life in the Caribbean."

"A rich corpse then?"

"Very. So, I'm still working on it. I have to come down in the morning and give a computer to Lisa and her crew to recover an erased disk drive. I could meet you at home, and we could then either take the weekend off or come back here and stay at the B&B honeymoon suite for free. We have it through Sunday."

"I would love to come up and stay at the B&B. We could even come back up tomorrow night. Why is Lisa working on the computer? Don't you all have forensic experts?"

"We do, but it's possible they erased the original

data, and the GBI lab is backed up for months."

"Lisa's great at doing that type of thing. She's talked about expanding the data recovery part of her business. Did the corpse erase it before he left town or was it an accident?"

"We don't know. It's a mystery. You're kind of thing."

"And Lisa's. She loves a mystery."

"Why don't you send me your ETA for tomorrow when you have it, and we can make definite plans."

"Counting the hours. Love ya'."

Derek hung up relieved that Megan was fine. He left to find out the status of the flash drive and to inform Tagger they needed another warrant.

Tagger stared at him, "The ticket was used? By Adam Cranford?"

"According to the CSR rep on the phone."

"Who used it?"

"I assume no one in the case left for the Cayman Islands on July 10th?"

"Not that I'm aware of. At least that narrows it down to a middle-aged man."

"Not necessarily. Lots of actors and actresses know how to use stage makeup to change their age, gender, and figure. People can even buy fat suits."

Tagger shook his head. "I thought this was a simple shooting. It's become something out of a sci fi novel, forget a mystery novel."

"The good part is that it can help us eliminate some suspects that we can prove were in the country that day after the departure time, unless they worked with a partner."

Tagger turned to his computer. "What day was the

10th four years ago? The 4th this year is a Saturday. So counting back, including a leap year, the 4th was on a Monday. That means the 10th was on a Sunday. The ticket was early morning meaning Adam planned to take off while everyone was at church."

"Sounds likely. He planned to arrive in the Cayman Islands 10 million dollars richer plus what he already had in his account. He was ready to live his dream."

Tagger continued to stare at his computer, "Instead he's shot dead on the 4th. I wonder if the 4th was significant."

"It certainly covered up the sounds of the shot unless someone used a silencer. And a stranger would not be noticed that night. Can you think of anyone who left that Sunday?"

"Off hand, I don't remember, but I'll ask around and do some calling. I'm sure Sharon and William were here because I asked them not to leave town. Mike would have been here also. Elizabeth only came back for the funeral, so she could have squeezed in a trip. But then why go there and return? Why not just keep the money here?" Derek said, "Good point. The same can be said for Tammy and her boyfriend and even Sam Vickers. Why use the ticket? For a vacation? Very risky. Why not keep the money and go later?"

Tagger mused, "Kind of makes me think there was a partner somewhere who got greedy."

"Business or romance?"

Tagger lifted up his hands. "As sneaky and shifty as Adam was, who knows? Maybe he had a love interest, because I don't see him sharing his money with a business partner. He did all the blackmail and theft alone. Also, the bribes. Maybe you were right about bringing in the French."

Derek raised his eyebrows, "How is that?"

"*Cherchez la femme*! Isn't that what they say in old movies? Look for the woman in the case."

Derek grinned. "Do you have any ideas on who she could be?"

"Not even a guess. She can't live in this county or everyone would know."

Derek said, "Maybe the computer holds the answer. If there's a woman, her information could be there."

Tagger nodded. "Maybe that's why it was erased. By the way, your flash drive showed only Adam's prints. There were partials of someone else but not enough to identify. So it's ready for you to take with the computer."

"Good. I'm leaving in the morning." Derek shared his plans with Megan to stay through the weekend. "I've been wondering if it would be useful to reconstruct the crime."

"Do you mean hire a forensic scientist who specializes in reconstruction? That's more than we can afford. Also, I don't think we have enough evidence for forensics."

"No, not to that level. If William and Sharon, as owners, would give us permission, we could have someone in Adam's office to gauge the noise and also the timing. Sam gave us his time frame of arriving at 10:00 p.m. and was only there for a few minutes. That means someone could have come during the fireworks or close to their ending, given the coroner's report. If it was towards the end, where was Tammy? Where were the others? How long would it take for someone to walk from the concert stage? What would Adam have heard and seen from where he sat? At this point, we have very little to go on. At least I haven't seen any notes in the case to that effect. I think it would help."

"We didn't do that kind of analysis. I guess it couldn't hurt. I'll talk to William. Did you have any more interviews planned for today?"

"Yes, Miss Wanda."

"The cleaning lady? You think she might be the love interest? She's in her seventies and chews snuff. She doesn't seem Adam's type."

Derek smiled. "I have some questions for her about what she saw. The notes describe her emotional reaction but not a lot of specifics."

"That's because all she talked about was how upset she was."

"I'm hoping she may have seen things that were not relevant to her but are to us. Is she still working, and does she still live in the area?"

"She's still alive, and I imagine she's working. She has a son who takes her money and wastes it, so she doesn't save for retirement. She also has a daughter who is married with a family, but they live in another county. Miss Wanda lives a few blocks from Adam's office. I'll give you the address."

Chapter 16:
Miss Wanda

Miss Wanda was a thin and petite elderly lady with dyed blond hair who chewed tobacco while she talked and then turned to spit it into a jar she carried. She was more than happy to talk to the cold case detective. She talked and talked and talked.

Derek, sitting on a sagging sofa in the tiny apartment, appreciated Miss Wanda and all the problems in her life and family, but he needed to rein her in to focus on the case. "So, you were expecting no one to be in the building that morning? It was a workday, wasn't it?"

Miss Wanda narrowed her eyes. "No, it was the 5th of July, and it was the Tuesday after a holiday. Most people took that day off too."

"I'm surprised if it was the firm's holiday that they didn't give you the day off."

"Tuesday's my day to clean their building. If they want it cleaned, that's the morning I have open. I go early before business hours though."

"I'm sure they value your reliability. Do you still clean there?"

"No, I don't want to work where I find people dead."

"Can you tell me a little more about that morning? For example, was the door locked?"

"No, I told the police that when it first happened. I had my key, but the doorknob turned when I touched it."

Derek had suspected Miss Wanda might have noticed details. Anyone who cleans the same place repeatedly usually notices anything different or out of place. "What about the inner office doors? Was just Adam's door open? And is that normal?"

"It was normal for the office doors to be shut but not locked. That morning his was open."

"Was that very frequent?"

"No, not really, maybe once every few months."

"What about the computer in Mr. Cranford's office? Was it turned on when you got there?"

Wanda stopped and thought. "Yes, it was and making a funny whirling noise. That was one of the things that scared me. The computer was alive, but Mr. Cranford wasn't."

"What time was that?"
"I always get there about 6 a.m. I vacuum, dust, empty the trashcans, clean up the sink in the break room and mop that floor."

"Do you know how to use a computer?"

"A little, enough to send emails, but my grandchildren do real well. They're eight and nine years old now."

"I was hoping you could tell me more about the computer. Did it make any sounds? Was anyone talking on it such as a teleconference meeting?"

"No, nothing like that. It was lit up, the screen flashing like car lights going through a tunnel at night. I thought Mr. Cranford was working and fell asleep. He was lying with his face on the desk, and his hands under his chest. I called his name, and he didn't answer so I reached over and shook him. Then I saw the blood and knew he was dead. I've seen other dead bodies. I used to work in a hospital when I was young."

"Was the computer still running then?"

"I don't know. I forgot all about it. I screamed and ran outside. I saw one of the officers going into the diner to get his morning coffee and waved and screamed until he came over."

"That's really helpful. Thank you. What about his desk? Were there papers on it?"

"No, it was clean except for him. That was unusual. Usually, he left some papers on it."

"What about the brown carved box that always set on his desk."

"Oh that thing. He called it his traveling box. I guess 'cause his great granddad had it or something. It was there."

"Was the lid open?"

Wanda thought a moment. "Yes, it was open. I think the key was in the lock which it wasn't usually."

"Was there anything else you noticed that was different or out of place?"

"The computer was usually pointing at Mr. Cranford's chair where he sat, but it was turned more towards the door. Tell you the truth, the whole thing was different and out of place."

"What do you mean?"

"Well Mr. Cranford sitting there. He always reminded me of a spider spinning his web and watching who he could snatch. Seemed real odd to see him as the trapped catch."

Derek agreed. And thought that was a good description of Adam.

Wanda continued, "His office was unusually clean. No files stacked up. Looked like he had already cleaned it. Like he was moving out or something."

Derek reflected that Adam may have cleaned out his office ready to leave, and it wasn't someone else who did the cleaning.

"I'm sure it was a scary experience, and I thank you for answering my questions."

"It was scary sure enough. Not that I missed Adam Cranford. He was someone I tried to avoid when I could. Always asking questions about my son and had he found a job. He knows my son is a creative person and doesn't do a 9 to 5 job like the rest of us."

Derek thanked Ms. Wanda and left. Why was Adam needling Ms. Wanda about her son? She didn't seem to have money to blackmail if he found something. Derek suspected it showed a side of Adam where he wanted to control for the pleasure of it, not just to make money. If there were other victims who felt belittled and otherwise threatened, that might open the suspect pool up even further.

Derek returned to the station just as the day shift ended. He walked to his office and made up a list of his notes and new questions. Finally, he locked up the evidence boxes and went back to the B&B. He wanted to think about Ms. Wanda's comments on the computer. What did that mean that the computer was still running? Had Adam started a process before he was killed that went wrong after his death? Had someone controlled it remotely? If so, why wait so late? What about the computer turned further towards the door? The box had been opened since Sam's visit, if they were both correct. Someone opened the outer door, walked up to Adam, who had to see the person, and shot him. If it was an enemy, he could have taken evasive actions or reached for a weapon. The notes said a small pistol was in his desk drawer but not used recently. He just sat there. Maybe the intruder was too fast or too well known?

Derek left work for the day, enjoyed a nice dinner, and a relaxing evening. Maybe tomorrow would have some answers.

Chapter 17:
Covert Clues

Derek drove straight to Lisa's office the next morning. She met him at the front door to sign him in and lead him upstairs to one of her computer labs. Derek explained about the flash drive.

Lisa said, "That's a huge help if we can recover the disk drive and compare the two sets of data."

Derek followed Lisa into a room with computers and long rows of tables. A young man sat at one of the tables. Lisa said, "Jackson, here's Derek with the erased laptop. Are you free to help me with it now?"

Jackson looked up. He was a young, thin man wearing glasses with fly away hair that gave him a classic geek appearance. Derek knew Jackson as the former IT director at the same church he, Megan, and Lisa attended. Jackson said, "Hi Detective Fielding. Sure, Lisa, I can stop any time."

Derek said, "Hi Jackson. Yes, we appreciate any help. Another mystery for you all to solve."

Jackson grinned. "That's Megan and Lisa's thing. I just look inside computers."

Lisa said, "And you do it very well. So, what's the story, Detective?"

Derek said, "First, I need you to sign this receipt

for me. As for the story, four years ago on 4th of July, a man was shot and killed in his office on the town square while fireworks exploded above the town. According to the cleaning lady, when she arrived at 6 a.m. the next morning, the computer was flashing like cars going through a tunnel. The forensic techs picked it up later that day and their lab sent it back with the note 'nothing found'. The Sheriff thought there was no useful evidence until I tried to boot it up this week. The entire computer has been erased of all data and software and just the operating system left on it hence the phrase, 'nothing found'."

"Wow," said Jackson. "That's seriously odd."

Lisa said, "I agree. If it was running at 6 a.m., there must have been some program on it. Any idea what he was doing on the computer before then?"

Derek said, "No. I leave that to you to figure out. Just for the record, the only fingerprints on the computer and the flash drive are the victim's. There are partial prints on the flash drive but not identifiable so no help."

"Mmmm," said Lisa. "Do you want us to just restore the data and download it to another drive for you to study or do you want us to search for certain information also."

"Whatever you can do will be a help. He had hidden bank accounts at State Bank where most of the money was transferred to an overseas account a few hours after his death. Any information on banking would be a particular help. Also he had a private email account he used to blackmail victims. It might say something like 'travel days' on it."

Jackson said, "Sounds like a seriously bad dude."

"He was."

Lisa signed Derek's receipt. "We will work on it today and see what we can find. Is Megan coming back today?"

Derek pocketed the signed paper. "Yes, we'll drive up to the B&B tonight and stay there for the 4th of July fireworks concert."

"Sounds nice," said Lisa as she walked him back out of the building. "I'll call you as soon as we have something."

Derek took the next item on his 'to do' list and drove to find the man who bought Freda's gun. Mr. Smith didn't answer the phone, and the house was vacant. A note to delivery people said to leave any packages inside the screened porch as they were on vacation. Derek wanted to question the man, but that would have to wait. Freda was falling out of favor as a suspect anyway, so perhaps his time was better spent elsewhere. He put his extra time to use and called an old friend who worked in special operations for a very hush-hush agency and asked her out to lunch.

Special Agent Phyllis agreed, and they met at a small cafe near her government building job.

"So, Derek, marriage looks good on you. How's Megan?"

"Very well. She's been traveling for her job and returns today. Maybe we can all get together for dinner one day when Frank is in town also. How's he?"

"Fine. Lots happening now with us both employed at the agency and a toddler starting to walk. Tell me what's going on. I'm sure you had a special reason for calling."

Derek grinned. "I did. I took a job as a cold case

investigator in a small town in north Georgia. At first glance, it was simple. A corrupt attorney shot dead at his desk late one night while 4th of July fireworks sounded outside his door. But the more I investigate, I'm getting some odd ideas and wondered if you could steer me in the right direction."

Phyllis tossed back her short blond curls and said, "Shoot. No pun intended. I assume it has to do with international crime since you called me?"

"Yes. After the attorney died, someone transferred his savings into an account in the Cayman Islands that he had already set up in his name and in which he was socking away money. Then a few days later, the killer or someone, used the victim's ticket and took a one-way trip to the Caymans and emptied out the account and was never heard from again. This person traveled on a middle-aged man's passport, but may not have been one."

"This person had some skills a local would not?"

"Exactly and since everyone close to the victim is accounted for now, they might have returned, or more likely the person using the ticket never came back. He or she is living somewhere enjoying at least ten million dollars and possibly much more in some foreign country or back in the States. My experience has never extended to international intrigue. With your role, you know more than I do."

"Spit it out, Derek. You're asking for my help."

Derek grinned. "No need to spit. I'm asking. How do I avoid being bogged down in a mass of conflicting agencies trying to follow this person? For example, the passport, who can quickly let me know if it's been used since that one time? I don't think the victim ever used it before. Also, what American agency best coordinates with the Cayman Authorities? And if we find a suspect, what is the process for getting to Interpol."

Phyllis bit into her sandwich and munched a moment. "You have a problem without knowing who used it. If you had a suspect, Interpol could help. As for passport fraud, the DSS, Diplomatic Security Service, investigates passport and visa crime. But to get the passport records you would request that from the US State Department. I think I can shortcut that path for you with some of my contacts. Is that on your wish list?"

"At the top of it. What about film at international airports after four years?"

"Sorry, not going to happen. However, the banking transfer would be simple, I think. No money laundering or tax evasion unless the IRS wants to make claims against the estate."
"We think that he raised most of it through bribes, blackmail, and stealing from his wife, so I imagine the IRS would like to know about it. but it's been four years and the estate settled with records gone."
"I imagine you're not short of suspects for this guy."

"Not locally, but when I put together the skills the killer had, I wonder. He or she stood several yards away and shot him once in the dead center of the forehead with a handgun, moved his money from a hidden account, erased everything but the operating system on the computer, and used his passport without being caught. Those skills require marksmanship, computer hacking, and banking knowledge and expert in makeup and disguise unless it was someone who looked like the victim."

Phyllis continued to eat as she thought about Derek's questions. Finally, she said, "You are thinking espionage training or military covert operations or maybe even ties to a foreign government."

"Sounds far-fetched, but yes. They stayed under the radar for four years until I tried to turn on his computer. And why use the passport in his name? Who wanted out of the country secretly?"

"No business partner or love interest?"

"None that we've found. There are a lot of crimes that could fall under various government agencies."

"True. The FBI investigates the cybercrime, white collar, and violent crimes as well as economic espionage. I'm sure you know that, though."

"Yes, Sheriff Tagger will contact them since it's a question of tracking down a wanted fugitive outside of this country. But I was wondering if any of our spy organizations are missing an employee? Someone who left the country on July 10th four years ago and never returned?"

"Ah, someone tempted by millions and gave into it? Someone your shady attorney encountered who used their skills to investigate him and uncovered his plans?"

"Exactly. Would anyone fit that mold?"

"I could see that happening. A small-town attorney unknowingly triggers an investigation of his finances overseas and then is used as an escape hatch for a life of ease. No one else knows about the money, so who will know if it's missing? Is that what you're thinking?"

"Yes, but how to find that person in so many agencies or the military with all the branches having undercover operations?"

"It's the type of thing you learn by word of mouth

and discussions at parties. A really clever operator might fake his or own death." She glanced at her phone. "Let me ask some quiet questions. I'm attending a social function tonight where I might encounter some knowing people. Especially, since it was four years ago and time for talk to go around about someone who just fell off the radar. Can you send me the names, dates, and other specifics to my encrypted email account?"

"Yes, of course. Appreciate the help."

"And I thank you for the lunch. Let's meet up when you and Megan have time."

"Agreed."

Derek paid the bill and walked back to his SUV. He wondered if he was letting his imagination run away, but there were so many things about this case that did not add up. He glanced at the clock on his dashboard and calculated that the restaurant for the mayor's alibi would be open now. So much better to show up for questions than make a phone call. He turned into traffic in a new direction.

The restaurant surprised Derek. He expected a cozy hide-a-way, but it was a very high-end business in an expensive neighborhood. Did the mayor have more money than expected, or had his friend offered a good discount? He walked to the employee entrance and knocked. It felt strange to no longer have jurisdiction in Atlanta after all his years on the homicide squad. His authority to pull someone in for an arrest without a warrant only applied to Stansboro County. He could arrest with a warrant outside his county, but in this case, he could do nothing today if Martin Sidingsly did not want to talk about his friend.

When a young man in a white chef's jacket opened

the door, Derek showed his credentials and asked to speak to Mr. Sidingsly.

"Sure, come on back. He's in his office. We aren't open yet, and I almost didn't open the door."

"I'm glad you did. I just have a few questions to ask him. Have you worked here for over four years?"

"Yes, but I was a sous chef then."
"Do you remember Andrew Harris and his wife Cece dining here? He's mayor of a small town in north Georgia. They tell me they eat here every 4th of July and other holidays."
"I seldom see the customers, just hear from them." The man grinned and added, "Hopefully it's 'complements to the chef.'" He knocked on a door and said, "Someone to see you from the police, boss."

A well-dressed and manicured man in his forties opened the door with surprise in his face. "Are you trying to be funny, Tony? Oh, I see. How can I help you?"

Derek again showed his badge and said, "A friend of yours has given you as an alibi for a particular night. I wanted to confirm that with you, if you have a moment?"

Martin raised his eyebrows. "Really? I can't imagine ... well come on in, and I'll see if I remember a particular time."

Martin sat down behind a very nice mahogany desk and motioned to Derek to sit in a comfortable easy chair. Derek explained again the dates and people in involved.

Martin grinned, "What? Did someone catch Andrew sneaking out of his little burg for the big, sophisticated city? Or do they think he has his hand in the till to afford my prices?"

"If you know the answer to the last question, please let me know. Otherwise, I want to know if Mayor Harris and Cece dined here on July 4th four years ago."

"Four years? Wow, let me think about it. They usually do come here on the 4th as Andrew doesn't like crowds and noise. Not sure why he went into politics."

"Can you say for sure about that 4th of July?"

"I'm fairly certain they did but let me check my reservation program. It will go back several years." Andrew turned to a computer monitor and typed for a moment. "They had reservations at 9:45 p.m. Can you mention why this is important?"

"His wife's brother-in-law, Adam Cranford, was shot that night in their hometown."

"Oh, yes, I remember reading about that, and Andrew discussing it. That was the night there was a major traffic snarl up on the interstate and many of my reservations were delayed. I mentioned to them they might have to take home some leftovers from the kitchen, and Andrew said he wouldn't complain. I can give them an alibi for part of the night. They got here at 9:45 p.m. and left about 11:30 or 12:00 p.m. because we visited over several glasses of wine. I hope that's helpful."

"Yes, thank you. If we ask you to sign a statement, would you be willing to do that?"

"Yes, but surely you don't think old Andy or even Cece, would shoot their attorney? Not very polite, you know. Andy's a bit of a wimp, really. Cece is not very dramatic, either."

"I can't comment on that. I have to follow up on

their story. Thanks for your time."

Derek did not consider Martin a very reliable alibi. He offered no proof except reservations that Derek could see on the screen. Everything else was his word. However, if Martin were telling the truth, that would let them out as his killer since they could not have finished and returned that fast.

Not a productive day in his search for clues as he struggled through traffic towards home. Perhaps Lisa and her team could find some answers. Still, he smiled. Megan should be home when he arrived.

Chapter 18:
The Computer

Derek made it home first and was setting down his suitcase when Megan walked through the door. She made straight for his arms. They agreed the two days had been very long ones apart and enjoyed their reunion before discussing practical matters.

Wise in the ways of Atlanta rush hour traffic, they decided to leave early and catch a late dinner before staying at the B&B. While Derek drove, Megan had a number of questions about the investigation. He filled her in with what he could.

She said, "It's an odd case. I mean, for a small town where everyone knows each other. It would make more sense in an urban environment with many strangers and computer whizzes working in tech companies."

Derek thought she nailed it. "Precisely, we're looking for a cold-blooded killer with both financial and surveillance skills and firearms expertise."

"Did Lisa say how long it would take to look at the computer?"

"She's offered to work tomorrow, if necessary, and will call. I had thought of doing a reconstruction of the crime on July 4th if William and Sharon approve it.

Sheriff Tagger is going to ask him."

"What do you hope to learn?"

"Logistics. What can be heard, seen, amount of time involved, that type of thing. Particularly how long it would take for someone near the concert stage to get to the office through the crowds."

"Are you thinking Tammy could have done it?"

"She's an unknown quantity. She's smarter than she acts and not shy about getting her way. She also has a boyfriend who teaches handgun safety and shooting."

"And she would have access to the office and his computer."

"Yes. Also, she could have found out about the hidden accounts. But the problem with her, and so many others in the case, is the fact someone left for overseas on the 10th. Would she come back and work for her uncle if she had gotten away with millions?"

"Probably not. It's the use of the passport that bothers you, isn't it?"

"Yes, that and the computer."

"Lisa will let us know. What are some places to eat a good dinner in town?"

Derek gladly turned to other conversation topics, and they had a pleasant evening with a nice dinner. No mention of cold cases until the next day.

After sharing the buffet breakfast at their B&B, Derek went to his office. Megan chose to tour the shops and visit businesses for an article she thought of writing on small town life. He met with Tagger and discussed their progress. William and Sharon had given permission for them to do a reenactment, and Tagger was contacting the FBI just as soon as Lisa got back to them. He said, "Better wait until we can say who used the passport."

Derek didn't comment. It was not his call. He understood Tagger's reasoning. He said, "One thought I've had is to talk to the people at State Bank again. I think it would be helpful to hear who made the changes Adam requested and what he said. Someone may have more information if he came in frequently. Also, a State Bank employee would have banking skills to carry off the theft. I don't know about the shooting, though."

Tagger agreed. "They had a sign on their door that the bank is open today but closed tomorrow."

"Maybe I can check with them then today."

An officer walked in escorting Megan. She said, "Hello, Sheriff Tagger. So nice to meet you again. We appreciated your help in catching the social media stalker."

Tagger smiled. "Glad to do it. In the future, if you get similar ideas, just let me know ahead of time what you're planning."

Megan smiled. Derek's phone rang. Lisa's name appeared on it. He answered, "Hi Lisa, this is quick. Just a moment, I need to check with Sheriff Tagger."

Derek put Lisa on mute and said, "I need to take this. I'll go back to my office."

Sheriff Tagger said, "Why don't you put her on speakerphone? It's fine with me if Megan listens." He turned to Megan, "Do you want to?"

Megan said, "Of course."

Derek unmuted Lisa and said to her, "I will put you on speaker phone. Megan and Sheriff Tagger are here."

He set down the phone as Megan and Tagger settled into their seats.

Lisa exclaimed, "Quick! You have no idea. This is

one dangerously hacked computer."

"What do you mean?"

"Whoever erased this computer was a top-level computer expert. It has a worm, a computer virus, written to destroy everything with the sophistication of governmental espionage. I mean we nearly infected our own lab, and we are prepared for malware."

Derek leaned forward, an intense look on his face, "What happened?"

"Fortunately, we have separate internet connections and keep computer systems isolated. We hooked this up and put in a flash drive to run recovery software. The worm took over and started erasing everything we recovered like one of those old Pac Man machines devouring everything in its way. We could not stop it no matter what we did. It infected our recovery software."

"Wow," said Megan. "Not the other computers?"

"No, we kept it isolated. But we lost all the data on the computer again, including our own software. We tried it again and booted up another recovery disk that downloaded each bit of data immediately before the worm was triggered and erased it. We got some, but not a lot. This worm is seriously bad malware."

"How did it get on there?" asked Sheriff Tagger.

"Probably through a flash drive. Someone wrote this code to do exactly what it's doing. That's why I said they have seriously sophisticated programming skills."

Derek asked, "Did you recover anything?"

"Yes, but not everything. We have some of his office files. We compared it to the flash drive and know that some are still missing unless he deleted them himself. The good news is we did find saved email from the personal email address you wanted and his password for it.

"That's helpful," said Derek.

"But there's more," said Lisa. "That flash drive backup was not clean. It has spyware on it that downloaded itself to his computer. Someone was spying on him."

"Maybe it was copied from his laptop onto the flash drive?" asked Derek.

"No, it looks like it was put on the flash drive from someone else's computer and then it downloaded itself onto the laptop."

"Strange," said Derek. "That indicates someone in his home or office or elsewhere had access to him if it didn't come from the internet."

"That's the way it looks. Someone he knew or visited was spying on him," said Lisa.

Tagger spoke up, "What was the point of this worm thing? Wouldn't it have been easier to just steal it and destroy the computer?"

"Good point. I think it was needed to make the offshore money transfers from his computer. The banks would have asked for text confirmations and email codes if a new IP address was used. After shooting him, maybe the killer didn't want to stay there or wasn't sure he would be able to take the time with the concert and unknown visitors coming by."

Derek said, "That would have been very likely. Adam already had one visitor."

Lisa continued, "As I said, this was a serious hack. Not only was there evidence of spyware controlling his microphone and built-in camera, but a listening device was hidden in the back of the computer. Anytime this computer was turned on or was near the victim, the hacker knew what was said and could see through the camera angle. If it was turned off, the hacker could still listen from the bug hidden in the back."

"Wow, who was this attorney? Some sleeper mole or super spy?" asked Megan.

"I don't know, but we did get the cloud address the hacker was saving the information to from the spyware. It went to a cloud account, but we couldn't get in with our password breaking software. In fact, it turned and started erasing the computer again. You need to keep this doomsday computer out of the public sphere. It belongs in a special isolation chamber or something."

"Agreed," said Derek. "I think it should go to the FBI and let their cybercrime division cope with it. I can come get it Monday."

"Good idea. Their experts might recognize the signature of whoever wrote this if they have come across his or her work before. All code has the signature of who wrote it like a novel shows its author's style. As for Monday, I have a better idea. Jackson and I were thinking of driving up for your 4th of July concert tomorrow and return that evening. We can drop it off for you."

Derek glanced at Tagger who nodded. "Yes, that would work well."

"In fact, despite its destructive skills for unsuspecting users, we talked about the value of plugging it back into the victim's office and seeing what it was instructed to do when back on that IP address. Of course, we'd disconnect the other office computers and monitor it. The operating system is still there and while the victim's data and programs were erased, the worm did not erase itself. Being plugged back into the same IP address might activate some built-in spy instructions after we do a quick restore before it erases again. It's worth a shot. That's, of course, if the current partner hasn't changed his internet provider. We can try to hack that cloud account it's storing to."

"Or give it to the FBI," said Derek.

"That too," said Lisa.

"Or do it as part of the reenactment," said Megan.

"Reenactment? That would be interesting," said Lisa.

"We call it a reconstruction," murmured Derek.

Tagger spoke up, "I would need to speak to the owner of the firm first. Why don't you go ahead and bring back the computer, and we'll see what we can set up."

Lisa agreed and disconnected. Derek shook his head. "Who around Adam had those kind of programming skills? Would his daughter just graduating from high school? Does his assistant Tammy? I think we're back to 'the unknown' again."

Tagger snapped, "Well, let's make him or her 'known'. I'm willing to try hooking up that computer if William agrees once he hears the risks."

While Tagger contacted William, the FBI, and pursued more warrants, Megan and Derek left to visit State Bank and learn more about their employees four years ago.

Megan said looking out the window, "This is beautiful country. It's hard to believe it's so close to Atlanta."

"Yes, I've enjoyed driving a few blocks and parking a few steps from my destination."

Megan laughed, "Yes, and easy for a killer to do so also."

"Actually, not on the 4th. The town closed the streets early in the morning."

Megan suggested, "Maybe that's why the killer didn't erase the computer until later? He or she had to take the time to walk back to their car, drive home wherever that was, and then do their computer instructions."

"Yes, that's a good point. I've been wondering why it was still running when Miss Wanda arrived to clean at 6 a.m. I doubt they would have taken the shuttle so some travel time must have been built in after the murder."

"What about the motor that your suspect, Sam, heard?"

"Something we can listen for tomorrow. What cars are parked nearby and where the sounds come from."

Derek's phone rang, and he answered through the car's Bluetooth. "Hi, Phyllis. Have you news? Megan and I are driving and rehashing our clues."

"Hi, Megan. Yes, Derek, I've sent you an encrypted email with what information I could glean."

Megan said, "Hi, Phyllis. I didn't realize you had been pulled into a small-town mystery. How are you and Frank?"

"We're fine. I hear you had an interesting investigative experience in a certain state this week?"

"How do you hear these things? Yes, it's been deferred for further review but interesting to know who is backing that legislation."

"Agreed," said Phyllis. "Derek, if you have questions let me know. I have to go."

Derek said, "Thanks for the help." Phyllis ended the call.

Megan said, "Do you think this killer is a foreign national or a spy?"

"I don't know, but the skill set makes me think of an agent gone rogue or a retired special ops agent."

"I wonder where Mr. Cranford would meet such a person."

"Adam Cranford is, or was, a man of secrets. I think the least interesting thing about his death was his murder."

Chapter 19:
Susan Weaver

Derek and Megan spoke to Ms. Forsythe. Derek asked, "Do your records show who set up Adam Cranford's accounts as he requested? I would like to speak to that person and find out more about his intentions."

Ms. Forsythe again turned to her computer, "I'm not sure our records will go back that far on the transactions but let me see." She gazed at her screen for several minutes. "It seems to be several employees that made changes. The ongoing transfers between the IOLTA and savings were made by Mr. Cranford on his home computer on the morning of July 5th. Susan is the teller who set up the automatic payments on the safety deposit box at Mr. Cranford's request. He did it by phone. It was done a few weeks before the 4th at Mr. Cranford's request."

"What about the transfer to his Cayman Islands account."

"The last one was made by Mr. Cranford from his home computer."

"Were any made from the tellers here?"

"No, he did those himself, at least the ones I have access to from this screen."

"Is Susan still working here? I'd like to ask her some questions."

"No, she left some time ago. She was a college student working until that fall semester. I can give you her full name, Susan Weaver. She was a very nice girl and was always very helpful with the customers. We were sorry to lose her."

"Do you know where to find her now?"

"No, we sent her end of year tax forms to her email also mailed to a PO Box here in town."

"I wonder if she's still here?"

"I don't know. She started working her last year in high school and then left for college, which was in another state. I think it was New York or some Northern state. We ran a background check on her and have her prints on file. Everything was clean. No criminal charges or convictions."

Derek nodded. "It was a long shot. She might not have noticed much."

Ms. Forsythe said, "I understand. In fact, there's only three of our tellers here now who worked four years ago. We have a lot of turnovers because it's an entry level job. We hire a lot of college students."

Derek started to stand and said as an afterthought, "When did she quit?"

"The date listed here is July 5th four years ago."

Derek sat back down. "That's early for a fall semester. Did you speak to her when she quit? What did she say?"

Ms. Forsythe continued to read the notes. "She sent an email saying her mom was sick, and she needed to stay home and help her. She asked if she could still use us as a reference and we said yes."

"Did anyone ask for a reference?"

"I don't see it in the notes."

Megan asked, "What did Susan look like? Was she thin, tall, fat, short, or attractive?"

Ms. Forsythe thought for a moment. "She was rather average in weight. Taller than I am, but I'm rather short. So, maybe she was average height. She was very bright and quick to learn. She had a pleasant personality."

Derek asked, "Is there anyone still working here who also worked with Susan? Perhaps they could tell us a little more about her so we could find her?"

Ms. Forsythe looked around the room. "Sheila worked here then. She was a teller until last year. Now she's a loan officer. Let me check and see if she has a moment to talk to you."

Derek tucked Susan's information he'd written down in a pocket. Ms. Forsythe entered with Sheila who looked to be in her thirties with short, styled hair and a plump figure. The two women sat down in chairs across the desk. Derek explained their interest in Susan and asked, "Did Susan talk to you about her background or family? We would like to find her."

"A little. She said she needed to earn extra money for college that fall. She had a full scholarship for her tuition and board, but it didn't cover things like food and extras."

"Did she mention which college she would attend?"

"No, she seemed to look forward to it a lot and was very excited."

"Did she ever mention meeting any of the customers outside of work? Or was she very friendly to any customers?"

Sheila looked down and seemed to think for a moment. "It's been so long, and we have a lot of turnovers with tellers. I don't remember her mentioning it, but I did notice she was very polite with the older customers. She was good at listening if they spoke much. I thought that was a good trait in someone younger."

"Yes, I'm sure it is."

"Oh, there was one thing I noticed. She was very quick to pick things up and seemed to understand our rules quickly. We didn't have to repeat them, and she was good with the software we use."

"Do you remember your customer, Adam Cranford?"

"Was he the man who was shot? I vaguely remember him coming in, but he didn't speak much, just smiled. He sometimes reminded me of the cat who swallowed the canary."

"Would you remember if you heard him ask to set up automatic transfers between his accounts?"

"Sorry, I don't remember that request. If that's all, I need to get back to work."

Derek said, "Yes, thank you." He turned to the bank manager, "Ms. Forsythe, I think we'll need to get her information such as fingerprints, so we'll be asking for a warrant."

"I understand. We're glad to help."

Megan and Derek walked outside. Megan asked, "Do you think it's a coincidence she quit that week? She doesn't sound like a hard-boiled killer if she's that young and was on a full scholarship to college."

"Coincidences do happen, but since she's the bank

teller who set up Adam's automatic safety box payment and could see the Cayman Island transfers. That's suspicious."

Megan asked, "Could she have used his passport? Could a young girl of average weight and height pass for a middle-aged short man?"

"I've seen some amazing disguises for the face and weight, but height is hard to change. On the other hand, her average height for a woman might match his short height for a man. The question is where would she learn her skills in shooting a handgun?"

"If she was in a military family, could someone have taught her about guns?"

"If she was in one." Megan raised her eyebrows and said, "So, the answer is to investigate Susan?"

Derek opened the car door for Megan. "Another mystery. Yes, I'll add her to the list."

As soon as they were settled in the SUV, Derek tapped on his phone. "I have the software to open Phyllis's' email. Let's see what she has to say." He spent a few moments reading, and then said, "She offers details, but, in summary, she has given me two names. One is of a man named Sergio about ten years older than Adam and also about his size and weight. He disappeared four years ago on a trip to Savannah, Georgia. His job was to do audits on nuclear power plants and certain government contractors. They suspect he was a double agent. He either escaped or someone took him out."

"He would love ten million and a passport with a prepaid ticket. And he would understand banking procedures," commented Megan.

"Yes. The other possibility is a woman named Amber in her twenties who had training in military intelligence but was dishonorably discharged for sociopathic tendencies. She stalked and threatened her ex-boyfriend's new girlfriend and hacked the woman's social media accounts. Amber put her rival's personal information on the web. She also sent images of violent death to the woman when she hacked her computer. Amber is of average height, weight and looks. She disappeared after the discharge which was about five years ago."

"Mmmmmm. She has computer skills and training in weapons, but what about banking?"

Derek turned off his phone and started the car. "No mention of banking. However, Phyllis sent their fingerprints and basic history. I'll check with Tagger and see if their fingerprints match any his experts found."

"I bet the killer wore gloves," said Megan.

"I wouldn't take that bet," replied Derek. "I'm sure you're right."

Returning to Stansboro, he dropped Megan off at the library to research the area's history for her article. Having learned the ways of obtaining a warrant quickly in Stansboro County, Derek soon had his warrant for Susan's human resource file, background checks, and fingerprints that day. So, he gave his new info to Tagger and began his own investigation into Susan's background. He was surprised to find she grew up in Lahillsville and was one year older than Elizabeth Cranford. According to his research, she won a full scholarship to study computer science at Carnegie Mellon University, one of the top schools for computer science. Her father and mother still live in Lahillsville. The father had several domestic violence arrests on his record. The mother had a disability of some kind.

Derek sat back in his chair. Obviously, another visit to Elizabeth would be necessary. But where was Susan now? Had she graduated? How advanced was she in computer science four years ago? Why would she spy on Adam and shoot him if she had a full scholarship to one of the most prestigious computer colleges in the country? He found no mention of shooting skills and no gun was registered to her or her parents.

He called Susan's college and after several long waits and transfers to one department or another, he found an administrator who could answer some basic questions. He was surprised to learn that Susan Weaver was not on record as having been a graduate or even a student of the college. Nor were any variations of her name in the last four years. What happened to Susan Weaver?

Tagger found the information interesting when Derek found him in his office, but not as much as one of the names given to Derek by Phyllis. Tagger said, "Sergio, the missing auditor, was in Adam's office at some point. His fingerprints were found on one of the legal pads in Adam's desk drawer. It's a handwritten note with the man's name and address on it. The handwriting is not Adam's, Tammy's, or William's."

Derek said, "So the inference is that Sergio wrote his name and address on the tablet and gave it to Adam who put it in his drawer?"

"Correct, but no date to know when this happened."

"Looks like we'll need the information Lisa found on Adam's flash drive as well as a glance at his paper files for the man's name."

Tagger said, "We can also show his picture to Tammy and William to see if they recall him. The man disappeared about the same time as Adam was killed, but they aren't sure of the exact date. He spoke to his supervisor in late June by phone over an audit he was pursuing that had irregularities on a government contractor. I've contacted the agency he worked for and hope to hear back soon."

Derek asked, "What about Susan? She's not appearing in the databases with current information, and her college has no record of her attending, yet she had a full scholarship to the most prestigious computer science degree college in the country."

"I agree, that's of interest but let's pursue Sergio's lead first and see what we discover. If you have time, speak to Elizabeth first about her. These students keep in touch on social media from all over the world. She could tell you if Susan went somewhere else or got married and chose her husband's name before we devote time and energy to her."

Chapter 20:
Sergio and Tammy

At that moment, an officer knocked on the door to let Sheriff Tagger know that Freddie and his attorney and also Tammy were at the front desk.

Tagger's eyes lit up. "Ah, not a waste of time. Tammy can answer some questions."

"You don't want to speak to Freddie?"

"No, but I will, or rather you will since you've brought him here with his attorney."

"He doesn't have an alibi, and he's an excellent shot."

"And a whizz at banking?"

"He now has a degree in forensic accounting, but I don't know his skills four years ago."

"Your points are well made. Let's go talk to them."

Freddie and his attorney were left to wait while Tagger asked Tammy to step into an interview room.

Tammy glanced at Freddie and then at Tagger, "Why me? I just came with Freddie. Do I need an attorney, too?"

"You can always have an attorney with you, but I want to ask you to identify a photo."

Tammy shrugged, "Oh, well, then sure."

Derek did not think a woman who so skillfully

handled Adam was in danger of police intimidation. He was right.

Tammy settled into a chair on one side of the table. She said, "I don't have a lot of time, but I'll be glad to help if I can."

Tagger grinned. "I appreciate your kindness." He slid a photo of Sergio across the table. "Have you seen this man in the office?"

Tammy peered at the photo. "Maybe. He looks familiar."

Tagger slid across the paper pad sealed in plastic but showing the man's handwritten contact information. "What about this?" Tammy raised her eyebrows. "Yes, I do know this person. He wanted to see Mr. Cranford who had been avoiding him."

"What do you mean by 'avoiding'?"

"This man, Sergio with the last name I can't pronounce, said that Mr. Cranford had not returned his calls. He wanted to speak to him. I suggested setting up an appointment, but he said he was only in town for that day."

Tagger leaned forward, "What happened after that?"

"Nothing. He reached in his pocket to leave a business card, but said he was out so I handed him a legal pad. He wrote his name and contact information on it. When Mr. Cranford came back to his office, I handed it to him and said Sergio asked him to call him. He laughed and said 'not if he could help it' and threw the pad in his desk drawer. He shut it and said if Sergio came back to tell him we couldn't help him."

"Did he come back?" asked Derek.

"Yes, late in the afternoon."

"What was the date?" asked Tagger.

"It must have been late June, maybe a week or two before Mr. Cranford was shot."

"Can you narrow the time?" asked Tagger.

Tammy thought for a moment. "I think it was on a Friday because I thought Mr. Cranford had already left for the weekend, and he came back in about 4 p.m. Sergio came back about fifteen minutes after Mr. Cranford arrived. I guess it was Friday, the week before Mr. Cranford was shot."

Tagger smiled. "Thanks, Tammy. That's very helpful. Did the visitor seem upset or angry with Adam?"

"Not angry like some of his clients. He seemed sort of amused."

"Amused?" asked Derek.

"Yeah, sort of like Mr. Cranford himself. Like the cat that ate the canary. This man seemed real confident."

"Was William also there?" asked Derek.

"No. It was just me. I wanted to leave early for the weekend and thought he was going to be a new client with lots of extra paperwork."

Derek confirmed, "So, he never spoke to Adam?"

"Oh, yes he did."

"I thought you said that Adam didn't want to see him."

"He did, but he made me mad. When Sergio came back, I showed him to Mr. Cranford's office and opened the door. Mr. Cranford didn't have another exit from that room."

Derek stared at Tammy for a moment and

reminded himself not to underestimate her in this investigation. "So, what did Adam do?"

Tammy shrugged. "He was just like he always was. He smiled that sly smile and said I must have misunderstood that he was leaving for an appointment."

"And then..." prompted Derek.

"Sergio said, 'No problem. I won't take up your time, Mr. Cranford. I only have a couple of questions about an audit I'm doing and some checks sent to you. I'm sure you keep excellent records and can help me. I don't think you want a subpoena.' After that, he shut the door behind him. I can't hear through it, so I left."

Derek asked, "Did you see him leave?"

"No, I left for the weekend while they were still talking."

Tagger thanked Tammy who left. While they waited on Freddie, Tagger asked Derek what he made of Tammy's information.

"If he was an auditor for government agencies and contractors, perhaps he was following an audit trail to Adam? Some payoffs not explained by the books by a company that did business with the county also?"

"Or maybe Sergio had discovered Adam's schemes and wanted to blackmail the blackmailer?"

"But in that case, why shoot Adam? That would remove the source of income."

"Could be he had all he needed to steal the money and just needed to eliminate Adam. He could easily have used the passport and ticket."

Derek said, "The answer could be in his audit job at that time. Have you contacted his supervisor?"

"I've tried. She's on vacation this week, but someone from his office is supposed to be contacting me today."

Freddie and his attorney walked in. Tagger asked several abrupt questions that resulted in Freddie finally coughing up an alibi. He had been sitting with an old girlfriend and her parents at their picnic in the park while Tammy was singing in the concert. Freddie wanted to avoid Tammy's wrath, not the law, and was looking for assurances it would be kept confidential. Tagger promised him nothing of the sort but did say without a legal reason nothing would be divulged. Freddie shrugged and left with his attorney.

Tagger called the old girlfriend's parents, whom he knew. They both came on speaker phone to confirm that Freddie sat with them from 9:00 p.m. until after the concert ended and then helped them carry their things back to their car. He did leave a couple of times to go to the restroom or speak to someone, but not for long. He left with some friends after the fireworks display. No, they didn't remember when he left for short breaks. Tagger thanked them and hung up.

He looked at Derek and said, "That probably does let him out if we can show he didn't have the time to get to Adam's and back through the crowds. I also checked on Tammy. She was with the other concert singers until about 15 minutes after the fireworks started. Then she left after it to find Freddie. They met up after the display. She doesn't have an alibi from leaving the concert to the end of the display, but she would need to push her way there and back through the crowds."

Derek nodded. "We can check out their travel time at the reconstruction. If they are out, that leaves Sergio and Susan as our best options."

"I haven't ruled out the original suspects, and we

also have Sam, but I agree the money doesn't fit with him leaving it there."

Tagger's phone rang and he said to Derek, "This is Sergio's office." It was the head of the agency as the supervisor could not be reached on vacation. Tagger said, "Thank you for calling back on a holiday. Let me put you on speaker phone with our cold case detective."

After Tagger explained the situation and Tammy's explanation, he asked, "Was your office investigating Adam Cranford?"

A gravel-voiced man who sounded in a hurry said, "No. Sergio was an auditor, not an investigator. He would have turned that over to someone else. I don't know why he was there, unless it was to clarify something he found in an audit."

Derek asked, "Would he have actually visited someone?"

"If he couldn't reach him otherwise, he might. From what your witness said, I'm wondering if he couldn't reach Mr. Cranford on the phone after many tries, so he decided to stop by while he was in the area. He might do that."

Tagger asked, "Can you tell us which companies or agencies he was auditing?"

"I've looked it up as I thought you might ask. He had several audits ongoing but in late June his notes show he was auditing a supplier by the name of Fenwood Corporation based in Savannah. The CEO is a man named Darren Fenwood and his brother, Barry Fenwood, is the CFO. They provide industrial cleaning supplies and services on a large scale. Both are veterans who have a history supplying our military and government agencies."

Derek asked, "Fenwood? Adam had a client named Fenwood, but I believe the first name was female, Dorothy, who lived in Savannah. She was arrested locally for drug possession and domestic violence a year before Adam was shot."

"Let me look at the other family members in the company...." Derek and Tagger waited. "I don't see a Dorothy as involved in the business, but Darren has a daughter named Dorothy. Let me do a little quick research....yes, she does have a criminal record and has been in and out of jail. Her problems in your county were more than drugs. She was accused of shooting her boyfriend but denied it. Looks like Mr. Cranford got her off the charge or it was not pursued."

"I can look that up. It was before my time as Sheriff, but I don't recall her name mentioned. Adam may have hushed it up. If he stayed true to form, he would have kept any proof and blackmailed his client. That would explain her fingerprints on a gun he kept."

"In that case, it would be her father paying blackmail. She is not rich. I'll ask the current auditor to look into that audit and see if there was a question about payments. Perhaps they were paying through the company as a business expense they didn't explain sufficiently, and Sergio was looking for more documentation."

Derek said, "Possibly. But if Sergio were not doing his job and somehow found out about Adam's schemes and absconded with the money and left the country in July, why did he not disappear until mid-July?"

"He may have disappeared earlier. We had emails from him and text messages but can't find anyone who saw him later than late June. In fact, his visit to

Cranford's office could be one of the last known sightings. He sent his supervisor, who has since retired, a text saying he was back in Savannah and working from his beach house. His family were still in Atlanta then. When they came down for the 4th of July, he wasn't there. His phone stopped transmitting at his beach house, and his car has not been found."

"That's odd," said Tagger. "Could he have been a victim?"

"We considered that but no evidence of a break in. His parents grew up in Russia and immigrated here. He was born here and is an American citizen. But of late years, he has started traveling back there to visit family. There were rumors of a Russian girlfriend. We thought he might have decided to move there and abandon his family in this country. In fact, we investigated him for espionage but have found no proof. "

"What about missing money? Did he take any with him?" asked Derek.

"Not according to his wife. However, given your suspicions regarding the shooting of Adam Cranford, I'll take another look. I assume you think he shot the man, stole his money, and then used his passport and ticket?"

"That's a possibility. He meets some of the requirements. He would know firearms and have some skill, knows finance and banking, and computers."

"How so know computers?"

"Enough to infect it with spyware and then spy on our victim."

"I'm not sure Sergio had those types of computer skills. He worked a lot with financial software but not cybercrime or identity theft. Although he was trained in firearms and banking practices, he was basically an accountant."

"Someone left the country on July 10th four years ago with Adam's passport and ticket. Was Sergio heard from after that?"

"Not from his family or employer. There was such a strong belief that he ran away to Russia that we didn't pursue it with no evidence to the contrary. If there is the chance he committed homicide, then we'll need to re-open the investigation and start an international search."

Tagger said, "We'll look further into Adam's contacts with the Fenwood family. It could be that Sergio is a victim if he uncovered a blackmail scheme or maybe even embezzlement."

They ended the call on mutual agreement for further investigation. Tagger said, "I'd like to look at those Fenwood documents myself. I vaguely remember the name. The other gun in his safety deposit box had her fingerprints but the statute of limitations has run before his death. But what I find odd is that there is so little about her in our system. Did Adam manage that?"

Derek said, "I need to meet Megan shortly, but I can fit in a visit to Elizabeth if she could see me now."

"Sure. Why don't you all have a nice evening? We'll meet up with your computer friends tomorrow morning?"

Derek smiled. "You'll have no argument from me." He called Elizabeth who agreed to meet with him and then texted Megan on his way out of the building. He could have asked Elizabeth over the phone about Susan, but he liked to look his suspects and witnesses in the eye. He could tell so much more about body language and speech nuances in person.

Elizabeth appeared the same as when he visited her last time, except her husband was not home. That suited him fine. She led him to chairs in the comfortable den area. He handed her a photo of Susan from the bank to be sure they were discussing the same person. "Is this a photo of Susan Weaver that you went to school with?"

Elizabeth looked at the photo. "Yes," she said a bit warily and cautiously. "Why do you ask?"

"I understand she worked at State Bank her last year of high school and the summer before leaving for college."

Elizabeth's face cleared of suspicion, "Oh, yes she did. She worked there. That was who I met lunch with our last year in high school. Did she know Dad?"

"I don't know. I wanted to ask her. Did you keep in touch with her?"

Elizabeth wrinkled her face and then opened her eyes in surprise. "No, I didn't. I hadn't thought about her for some time. I should have. I lost touch with several of my high school friends in college, and especially after I got married."

"Do you know where she is or how to get in touch with her?"

"No, but let me see if we're still connected on our social media apps." Elizabeth walked over to her laptop and began to type while Derek stood behind her and watched the screen and her keyboard.

"No, she's not on any of my current social media. In fact, she's closed them or someone did. That's odd. Susan was a whizz at computers. She was one of my computer club members."

"Is that the same one that met at your parent's house?"

"Yes, we met in the library when Dad wasn't working. Otherwise, we met in the living room."

"Did Susan know your dad?"

"Sure, all my friends did, but he wasn't around a lot. I mean she would know what he looked like, and he would know her. I never saw them speak except to say hello."

"Do you still have a phone number for her?"

"Yes, let me write it down for you."

Derek took the paper and phone number. Then he dialed the number. "It's been disconnected," he said.

Elizabeth shook her head. "I don't know how to reach her, then. I can try some of our old friends or you could check with her parents. They still live here, I think."

"I will." Derek sat back down as Elizabeth moved away from the computer to her chair. "Can you tell me about your computer club? What did you do and what did you discuss when they met here?"

Elizabeth gazed at the ceiling and flipped her ponytail with her hand as she appeared to think. "We had to have a certain grade to be accepted. We met and discussed things not taught in class such as new tech developments, software programs, and how to write code. We tried to create our own apps such as one for our class to sign up as a group to network. Unfortunately, the apps we did mostly didn't work or had bugs. We didn't have the time to really develop them."

"Did you ever use spyware or malicious code?"

"I'm sure we discussed it, but that was not a club project."

"Did your dad leave his computer in the library

when you all met there?"

Elizabeth gasped, "Do you think Susan did something to his computer?"

"I don't know. I'm trying to find out who was around it."

Elizabeth stopped pulling her ponytail. "I can't remember it being there when we were meeting there. Usually, Dad had it with him. I guess it's possible, though."

"Can you tell me about Susan? What was her personality?"

Elizabeth rolled her neck. Derek got the impression deep thought outside of technical matters was not something Elizabeth liked to do.

She said, "Oh, I guess she was OK. She was the friend I was thinking of when I mentioned having an abusive father. I think her father hit her and her mother. Susan came in a few times with bruises but wouldn't talk about it. And she would get really angry suddenly if someone took something of hers or wasn't very polite. I guess, I thought she left town to get away from her dad and just didn't come back. She was very funny at times and then could be very sarcastic. I remember she was thrilled at being accepted at Carnegie Mellon for their computer science program. But she worked really hard to get it. I assumed she must have a great job and forgot about us."

"Did she have other hobbies like hunting or acting?"

"She was in the drama club and also played soccer, but I never heard her mention hunting."

Derek stood and thanked Elizabeth.

She also stood up and said, "Susan was angry at

times, but I can't see her shooting anyone if that's what you are thinking she did. She wasn't physically violent. Besides I don't think she even knew Dad other than meeting him here."

Derek thought a thief did not need to know their victim well but remained silent. He thanked Elizabeth again and left. She promised to try and find Susan's contact information.

Derek walked out to his SUV. He didn't have time to visit Susan's parents tonight, but he would tomorrow. He cleared his mind of murder and met Megan for dinner. She debated on the best place to eat in a town with so few restaurants. Derek had no strong feelings on the subject as long as he ate. They settled for a restaurant a couple of blocks from their B&B that gave them a chance to stroll around the town square area and become familiar with the area.

Megan said, "I agree with you. It's hard to believe no one saw someone enter Adam's office. It's a very open town square, and his door is right in the middle of one side. There had to be dozens of people roaming around."

"The fireworks were in the opposite direction, so people would have been facing away from his location."

Megan said, "Still, sometimes people leave early, or children or pets decide for them."

Derek said thoughtfully, "True. It's possible someone did see the killer."

"And?"

"And they liked the killer and didn't like the victim."

"Ah, such as a well-loved wife or law partner?"

"Yes. I think either of those would qualify. Also, a realtor who is one of their own and trying to defeat a smelly plant."

"In that case, we may never know."

"Oh, we just have to follow other leads. Also, tomorrow night we can see how easy it is to view the office door."

Megan agreed, and they set aside further theorizing for the rest of the evening. They enjoyed walking in the deepening dusk, the sound of crickets, and the rustle of birds settling down for the night. Their discussion moved on to the remaining months of summer and Derek's law school plans.

Chapter 21:
Independence Day morning

The next morning brought a day of bright sun and cloudless skies, perfect for picnics and fireworks.

While Megan enjoyed some after breakfast time to rest in the B&B's porch swing and catch up on her reading, Derek drove to Susan's parent's home. He knocked on the door, but no one answered. A battered pickup truck sat in the cracked and crumbling driveway. The house also looked as though it could use some tender loving care. Built in the late 1930s or 40s, someone had remodeled it about 30 years ago. Now shingles were missing from the roof. The once white paint was cracked and flaking off. It stood out from its neighbors where similar older houses showed recent paint or mowed lawns.

Derek pulled out his phone and called the number he had found for Susan's father, Richard Weaver. No answer. He started to walk away when the door opened.

A man about fifty stood in the doorway wearing a worn t-shirt and jeans. His eyes were blurry, and he had not shaved in several days. "Who are you, and what do you want?"

Derek introduced himself and showed his badge as he walked back up the steps. "I am looking for your daughter, Susan. Can you tell me how to reach her?"

The man barked a short laugh. "No! And I don't care where she is. Get lost." The door slammed shut.

Derek raised his eyebrows. Not a helpful citizen. Maybe the reason Susan had not returned was clear. He put his search for her on the backburner until after this weekend. He would then try to find Susan's mother, as well.

He returned to the B&B to find Megan sipping iced tea on a hot morning and waving to him from a wide wooden porch swing. She swung gently back and forth with an unread book in her lap.

Derek grinned and walked over to her. "Enjoying yourself?"

"Very. I'm afraid my new book is remaining unread, though. How did your visit with Susan's parents go? Did you find her?" Megan shifted over so Derek could sit beside her.

Derek sat down gingerly on the old swing, hoping it would hold his weight as well. "Not well, and no. The father said he didn't know where she was and slammed the door in my face."

"Not a happy family picture. Poor Susan. I wonder if she left an abusive family to start a new life? Sometimes people do that. Part of their healing is a complete break with their past."

Megan turned to lean against Derek, and he put his around her as the swing gently swung back and forth.

"Maybe, but Susan is a mystery I need to solve at this point. What are your plans for the day? Are you planning to join us when Lisa and Jackson arrive?"

"I'd like to do so. Am I allowed to take part in the reenactment?"

"Tagger has said you can. We tried to keep William and Sharon out of it, but William insists he needs to be there for liability reasons. Sharon wants to be with William. Since we can't legally force them to do this at this stage in the investigation and it's their property, we can't keep them out."

Megan said, "Maybe they want to make sure you don't find anything?"

"Maybe. And now it looks as though Tammy will need to be there to help us set up the furniture in Adam's office since William doesn't remember."

Megan laughed. "It will be a party. Should we serve hors d'oeuvres?"

"I don't know about food, but Tagger did make a comment about selling tickets."

"Not a bad idea. We could perform in the square. Or better yet, maybe it will be like those golden age mysteries where the suspects all meet in the parlor and the brilliant detective, that's your role, says who did it."

Derek grinned, "Fine with me if it works, but not all the suspects can be rounded up for our 'parlor' game. Although it would be nice if the killer shows up and says 'I did it,' if that's what you mean by old fashioned endings."

"I guess that only happens in books and movies." Megan took another sip of tea and said, "It's going to be a hot day. I'm already sweating, and I'm not in a crowd walking around. Have you thought that maybe someone just wanted an air-conditioned office, found Adam counting his money, and shot him to steal the money?"

"Yes, but that doesn't account for the computer shenanigans. Who stole it online?"

Megan sighed. "It always comes back to that,

doesn't it?"

"Yes, it's not a simple murder. And that is a detail Tagger and the techs did not have four years ago. It puts it into a different category."

"Maybe it's two people? One here that shot Adam, and a second person who committed the cybercrime?"

"That's a possibility I've considered, but someone who was nearby Adam put the listening device on his computer. It couldn't be a typical hacker, someone at a distance."

Megan sighed. "A mystery, indeed. Can I ask if you have a suspect?"

Derek pushed against the porch setting the swing to set gently swinging again. "The most obvious answer is a blackmail victim. That is who has the most motivation. Second down the suspect list is the wife or business partner, with the motivation of money or revenge. In this case, the wife had the money, and the partner was well off financially. If they wanted to marry, Sharon could have filed for divorce. If she had religious scruples against divorce, one assumes she would have even more scruples against shooting her husband in cold blood. Someone stealing Adam's secret money cache could be a motivation for murdering him, but once it's gone there was not a lot Adam could do about it. He couldn't report it as a crime, but if he knew the thief, he could seek the person out and retaliate."

"Do you have a name?"

"I have a couple of names in my mind, but I better not say at this point. I still feel there is the unknown, the *Personne Inconnue*, as they say, still to be revealed." Derek stopped the gentle swinging, and said, "I need to go to the station. What are your plans? I think Lisa and

Jackson should be here about noon."

Megan sat up and said, "I need to finish up some research on an article, so why don't I join you all after Lisa and Jackson arrive."

Derek kissed her goodbye and then left for the police station. He arrived to find Sheriff Tagger talking on the phone and busy with logistics for the 4th of July celebrations. In fact, it was a busy day for the Sheriff's department as they were in charge of making sure all went well with the large crowds and controlled mayhem for the holiday.

Derek started a search on Susan Weaver who seemed to have disappeared that July week four years earlier. He could find no indication she had shooting skills, but she certainly had computer skills. He had two ideas. One she is happily living overseas with several million dollars, or two, she somehow came across a murder and was a victim herself that evening. He didn't think her father would search for her, and from what he read, he suspected the mother would do what the father said. Her friends were all leaving for their own college experience and assumed she also took off. No one would miss her.

Just before noon, Lisa and Jackson arrived with the nefarious computer and one of their own computers to set up for the reconstruction for that evening. Megan joined the group. Derek discovered that Tammy had invited Freddie to help with moving the furniture. William and Sharon decided it was a good time for a late spring cleaning to clean out Adam's old office for reuse and move his papers to another unused room. Derek suggested that perhaps during the actual reconstruction, it would be best for them to be enjoying the fireworks outside.

Lisa and Jackson expressed a different opinion. After introductions, Lisa looked at Adam's old office and said, "I'm so glad you're here, Tammy. Can you show us how it was set up so I can get the angle right on the computer camera?"

Freddie looked at Derek, "Don't you also need to see the angle of the shot?"

Derek said, "The crime scene techs took measurements four years, but it would help to see it, yes."

Tammy nodded and said, "Well, his desk faced the door, and the file cabinets were on the wall next to the door. The computer set on the side table next to the main desk."

Derek asked, "Did he always keep his computer on that same table?"

Tammy said, "Yes, always."

Lisa asked, "If Jackson and I help, can you help us set it that way now?"

Tammy said, "Sure, but the file cabinets are heavy if you're going to hook the computer back up where it was. Freddie will need to help on that."

Derek and Megan also offered to help. With a group effort, the storage room became Adam's office again. Banker's boxes were removed, computer cables rerun, and WI FI passwords discussed. Lisa said, "Tammy, you and William must, absolutely must, remove every computer, smart phone, printer or device that runs on this system when we hook up Adam's computer."

"I will make sure Uncle William knows to do that with his phone, but why?"

"There's a virus on Adam's computer that erases everything it touches. We're putting a firewall around it as best we can, but we need to make sure all the passwords are the same as four years ago and then change everything after we do this test."

"OK. You better let Uncle William know."

"He knows. I've already spoken to him, but I wanted you to know also."

"This seems really kind of crazy. I mean what can you learn about setting up his computer? Especially, if it was erased?"

"We have software to restore erased data, although this virus keeps removing it on his computer. We discovered codes with instructions to send data to a cloud account from this IP address. I'm so glad you haven't changed providers."

"We only have one in this town, and we don't change the passwords. Everything's the same as it was that night."

"Great, we'll help you make your network more secure before we leave. That's what my company does is make businesses and individuals safe from cyber-attacks."

"Cool," commented Tammy.

Freddie asked, "When I studied forensic accounting, we had to go back and look at what had been done. Do you do sort of a history study of the computer?"

"Sometimes, but today we're just trying to duplicate the original computer set up to get the instructions started again. It's a long shot. May or may not work," Lisa explained.

Derek stepped out of the office to call Sheriff

Tagger. He wanted to make sure Tagger had found an officer to time the walk from the concert stage to the office this evening to check the timing of Tammy's and Freddie's alibis after the concert. Tagger was still busy with the 4th of July plans, but said he had someone and also someone to stand at the office door to keep out any curious visitors.

Derek stepped back inside to find William looking through client files while Sharon sat on a chair watching.

William asked Derek "What was the name you wanted to know again?"

Derek said, "Dorothy Fenwood is the name we're looking for. She was arrested but the charges dropped despite her boyfriend's claims."

William said, "I'll look again, but I didn't see anything with that name on it."

Derek looked at Sharon, "Does the name mean anything to you?"

"Adam never discussed his cases with me. Although, I think I remember the company name from one of Adam's businesses that went bust. Didn't they do cleaning or something? He used them because the brothers were veterans. One was in Marine Corps or something?"

Derek said, "The Marine Corps? That's interesting. Do you know which business?"

"I think it was the restaurant he invested in out on Highway 101. I don't have any of the business records."

"We'll check. The other owners may have them. Thanks," said Derek.

Entering into the re-enactment concept, Tammy and Freddie left the lights and shades as they had been that evening. Derek thought the re-enactment might be too detailed as it was mainly to check time on alibis, listen to the acoustics, and run the computer. However, better safe than sorry.

Megan looked up from vacuuming the carpet to clear out dust and bits of paper. "This is sort of creepy. I hope the killer doesn't actually show up again."

Derek grinned at her. "Oh, I don't know. I would like to talk to the killer, so I would be glad if he or she showed up."

Megan grinned back. "I'll let you interview him first before I get my story in that case."

"Are you writing an article on the murder? I thought it was about a small town's fight to remain friendly and neighborly despite Atlanta's outgrowing urban population."

"I think both are sellable. My ministry isn't interested in them for their media outlets, but our agreement allows me to sell freelance articles. I'm not sure about Adam's article if we can't get some sort of resolution."

"I hope we'll know more tonight," said Derek.

Chapter 22:
Independence Day night

Frankie and Tammy left to bring back sandwiches and pizza for the group. Derek could hear the sound of crowds growing outside. Lisa and Jackson set up their own computer next to Adam's that they had brought with them."

Derek asked, "How are you using the second computer?"

Lisa looked up at him from her chair beside the computer table, "We need it to capture what's showing on the computer and keep it intact. I'm not sure we need everything the same, but we do need the same computer set up that Adam used."

"I understand. I was thinking of the logistics of the camera pointing towards the door."

Lisa looked over at the office chair, "We can move over a little."

"Sounds good," replied Derek.

Finally, the original murder scene was recreated. Tagger had still not joined them, but the tired 'reconstructors' sat down to eat pizza.

Derek said to Tammy and Freddie, "Are you two planning to go to the fireworks?"

"Yes, we wouldn't miss it. No offence, but I don't

really care who shot Mr. Cranford. I mean it's not important to me, now."

Derek said, "No reason you should be here. I hope you both enjoy the fireworks."

He looked at William and Sharon, "Are you also going? There's really no need for you to stay, and I know your family is having a large picnic space reserved."

William smiled, "Oh, we wouldn't miss this. We see our families all the time."

Derek said nothing.

As they finished and cleaned up from the late supper, fireworks sounded in the distance and overhead. They grew louder. Derek opened the door and walked out into the square. At 10 p.m. darkness had finally fallen in the midsummer night. Megan followed him. She said, "It's so dark. That's why no one saw anything. I assumed there would be lots of streetlights like Atlanta."

Tagger walked up to them at that moment. He said, "No, we don't have lights on the square except what the offices and businesses have. Most are closed at night anyway, including the shops."

Derek said, "And most people are listening to the music and looking up at the sky. I see a few walking around, but it's hard to see them in the glow from single light bulbs and a few antique lamp replicas."

Megan said, "Maybe no one did notice the killer."

Tagger said, "We asked everyone over the news and on social media. No one ever came forward." He added, "I have someone trying to replicate both Tammy and Freddie's stated actions that night. I think the crowds are about the same, which is good. And everything is quiet for the moment, so I wanted to join you all."

They turned and walked back into the office. Derek said, "So far we've set everything up exactly as it was that night, at least as far as the furniture goes. Lisa says they're setting up the computer."

Once inside Derek glanced in at Lisa and Jackson who were immersed in their computers. William and Sharon sat in the reception area looking worried. Derek continued to look at the time. He said, "This is the hour when Sam arrived and left just before Adam was shot."

Tagger crossed his arms and glanced out the window and then paced around. He said, "OK let's re-enact. I'll step outside and enter." He walked out the door, turned around, and re-entered the reception area. The bell chimed on the door alarm. He walked towards the only fully lit office that was Adam's and stopped outside the door. He raised his arm and pointed an imaginary gun.

"Adam had to have heard the door, even with the outside noise. And that's a difficult shot. I'm not sure I could make it. You're right Derek. It has to be someone skilled in handguns."

Derek said, "I just learned today that the Fenwood brothers are veterans. One was in the Marine Corps. I imagine both of them have good shooting skills."

Tagger whistled, "That bears further investigation, then. Do they? Or were they supply clerks?"

Derek said, "Still, basic training."

Tagger nodded and looked again at the computer set up. He asked, "Why was the computer turned towards the door if Adam was sitting at the desk and was shot where he sat? He couldn't work at it like that?"

Lisa looked up and said in an excited voice, "I think we can help with that shortly. We reconnected everything and got it started before the virus took over. Hopefully, we can catch the spyware recording."

A voice said from the computer, "I'm sure you can. The video captured everything that night."

Lisa gasped. Derek, Megan, William, Sharon, and Tagger all jerked around to stare at Adam's computer. The screen showed a young woman smiling at them. Behind her was a dark background. She had short brown hair and wore a casual pink top.

Lisa said, "Who are you?"

Sharon exclaimed, "Susan! Susan Weaver, is that you?"

"Yes, Mrs. Cranford. I heard from a friend of a friend today that Livvy was trying to get in touch with me, so I called her. She told me what you all are doing. I'll be glad to help. Just for the record, I didn't kill your husband. She asked me if I did."

Derek stepped inside the computer camera range and took advantage of the shock still written on the others' faces. "Susan, I'm Derek Fielding. I'm the cold case detective trying to solve Adam's murder. If you didn't kill him, who did?"

"Well, I am not absolutely certain, but I can make a good guess. The thing is I spoke to an attorney today. He suggested I offer the information in exchange for a trade. You don't press charges against me, and I'll share the video I have."

Tagger quickly found his voice and stepped closer. "Only the D.A. can make a deal like that. You have a duty to tell us what you know."

Susan cocked her head on one side and appeared to

think. "I don't believe I do, if it's self-incriminating."

Derek spoke up, "You should be aware that anything you say can be used in court." Susan nodded, "I had a long talk with the attorney today. As I said, I want a deal. However, in the spirit of cooperation I will share information."

Derek asked, "Where are you?"

"In a foreign country."

"Where?"

"I'd rather not say. I will say that I have an ironclad, isn't that the word always used in police stories, alibi that I did not shoot Mr. Cranford. I was at the hospital that night from 9 p.m. until 2 a.m. My mother broke her arm, and I carried her to the emergency room. I sat there with her until 10 p.m. and then was with her while they examined her and x-rayed it and set it. It was a busy night with several car wrecks and fireworks accidents, so we waited a long time."

Sharon said, "Your poor mother. I haven't seen her in a while, but she didn't mention it. I do remember her having a cast at one time."

Susan said, "She had a broken arm because she tried to break up a fight between my father and myself. He pushed her down the stairs. She wouldn't talk about that."

"What were you fighting about?" asked Derek.

"Signing the forms to allow me to get the student loans to cover my non-tuition expenses. I had thought my room was covered in my scholarship, but I learned it was not. I needed a cosigner on my student loan. Dad refused and said he didn't want to be left holding the bag if I couldn't pay." Susan snorted, "Like I couldn't pay after getting a degree in computers at Carnegie-

Mellon. He was such an idiot."

"So, you were with your mother the whole time?" asked Derek.

"Yes, and when I realized what happened to Adam, I made sure to get a copy of the ER's film for that night. I was there most of the night, except when I went with her to x-ray. The doctors were also there."

"So, tell us about your computer hacking," asked Derek. "Did you put spyware and a bug on Adam's computer?"

Susan took a deep breath and said, "Yes, I did. I'm sorry Mrs. Cranford, but your husband was not a nice man. When we started meeting in the library for our computer club, I overheard him threatening someone on the phone outside the windows on the porch. He wasn't shouting like my dad, but he made it clear they must pay him or he would see them in jail. I got curious and listened. I started wondering what he was up to."

"Why didn't you tell us?" asked Sharon.

Susan shrugged. "I didn't know what it was, and I was learning spyware and hacking. Our group was really into that for a while, so I thought I'd write some code of my own and test it on his computer. Then I learned a lot about him and also added the bug on the computer. He was really dumb. He never noticed," snorted Susan.

"We had you in our home..." started Sharon but was spoken over by Derek.

"We understand. Maybe you wanted to help Elizabeth?"

"Yes, at first. Then I was really shocked. He was blackmailing people and even taking kickbacks. But as I learned more about the law, I realized I could also be prosecuted if I said what I had done. I needed money for college costs, so when I saw an ad for State Bank for a teller, I thought I could not only earn money for college but also find a legal way to catch Mr. Cranford. I had discovered his secret accounts."

"What happened on July 4th, four years ago?" asked Derek.

"Well, as I said, I went with Mom to the hospital. When we got back home about 2 a.m. I saw an alert on my computer. I had set it up to let me know if the computer was running. I was surprised it was at night. I was crying and exhausted, but I clicked on it. I watched the recording and saw everything that happened. I saved it to my cloud account and realized that since he had been shot, they would discover my spyware and maybe trace it back to me. I also had put that bug on his computer. I could erase the spyware from my home, but I had to go there to get the bug off. It was about 3 or 4 a.m. in the morning, and the streets were mostly empty by then, so I drove there."

Susan stopped and gulped.

"And," prompted Derek.

"And on the way, I started thinking. If he was dead and no one knew about that money, I wouldn't need a loan. I could use some of his secret money. I worked at the bank and could create my own offshore account. Then I thought about that ticket he hid in his wooden box. I thought why not get that and take a trip first? I studied drama and knew about how people could use make up and disguises."

Susan appeared to shake and took a deep breath. "When I got there, the door was unlocked, so I walked in. Mr. Cranford was dead and lying on his desk. I didn't want to get too close to him, so I turned the computer, so I could use the keyboard. I moved his money to his offshore accounts. It needed to be on his computer, and I had his passwords. I grabbed his ticket and passport from that wooden box on his desk. Then I inserted a worm I had written just in case I needed it on my flash drive that would erase the whole computer. I wasn't sure what computer forensics could still find even if I took off my spyware. Also, I didn't want to steal the computer as it needed to be there to complete the money transfers. It was just before daylight, and I needed to leave, so I left it running and went back home."

"Why didn't you use the money to pay for your college if that's why you got it?" asked Derek.

"I..I..I was going to, but I tried to get mother to leave Dad. She wouldn't. I realized she loved being abused more than she loved me. I just wanted to get away from everyone. I thought why go to college when I can use the whole 30 million."

"How much?" exclaimed Sheriff Tagger.

"Well, a lot. I transferred 10 million from his State Bank account, but he already had money there."

Derek spoke quickly, "So, who shot Adam Cranford?"

"Adam had evidently planned to get all the last blackmail money he could before he left town. He had more than one visitor that night. One of the men he was blackmailing was called Sam. He came first and argued with Mr. Cranford. He threw the money at Mr. Cranford and left. Then his next victim came in, but it wasn't the person he expected. He was waiting for a woman, but a man showed up. I couldn't see him from the camera. He stood outside the door in the reception area. But the video showed Mr. Cranford saying, 'Oh, it's you. Where's your daughter? Isn't she ready to make her last payment?' Then the voice off screen says, 'No, she's not. The statute of limitations has run. You have nothing to blackmail her with.' Then Mr. Cranford says, 'In that case, I guess it's your turn. I just had a long chat with a government auditor named Sergio this week. Boy, the things I could tell him about you and your company! I might still have those receipts from my restaurant that didn't match your books. Then there are those payments to me for your daughter you listed as legal consultations. That auditor wanted to know what kind of consultations a criminal attorney did for a business.'"

Derek asked, "Did he say he 'had' the invoices, or he 'might' have them?"

Susan thought for a moment. "He said he had them. Anyway, the man said, 'I've taken care of Sergio, and you're next.' Then suddenly in an instant, Mr. Cranford jerked and fell forward. I think I heard a pop, but it was hard to tell with all the fireworks. Anyway, the man then stepped into camera range and picked up the remaining money on the desk. He laughed and said, 'I'll take this as a refund, Adam.' He walked away, and I heard the bell on the door again. This must have happened during the fireworks when I was at the hospital, but I didn't see it until about 3 a.m."

"So, where is the video?" asked Derek.

"It was in the cloud storage with all the information I had on Mr. Cranford. Now I have it offshore in an account and on a flash drive to give to my attorney."

"And what do we need to do to get it?" asked Derek.

"I'd like to come back to the States. I haven't talked to my dad and don't want to, but I've spoken to my mom. She's not doing well. She didn't care much about me, but I'd kind of like to see her, and well, I miss my friends and being home. If you could agree not to press charges for the hacking and theft, I'll send the video."

Sheriff Tagger snorted. "There's a few other charges, but like I said earlier that is a decision the District Attorney would have to make. I will talk to him. How can we contact you?"

"I'd rather contact you. If you'll give me your number, I'll talk to my attorney. I'd like him to negotiate for me."

Susan disappeared from the screen. Suddenly it started flashing like cars going through a tunnel.

"Darn!" exclaimed Lisa. "She's started that darned worm again. It's erasing itself." She looked at Derek and grinned. "But Susan's not the only one that can video screens. I filmed her and recorded everything she said,"

Megan said. "So did I on my cell phone."

Derek said, "I noticed. Thanks to both of you."

"Amazing," murmured William.

A sob escaped from Sharon.

William hugged her. "So, none of us, Hon."

Sharon said, "I knew it. I knew it wasn't, but I couldn't imagine who else would want to shoot Adam. I never thought of two different people. And Susan was in our house as a friend! Who is the man she saw?"

Tagger said, "We can't say anything more about that. I have to coordinate with several law enforcement agencies because this has become international. The D.A. may offer her a deal, but we need to find her."

William said, "It's been a long day today. I suggest we leave everything as it is except what you have to put back in your evidence room. I'll going to leave the furniture as it is. It's time to redecorate that room and for me to look for a new law partner."

At that moment a young female officer came in the outer door. She said, "I finally made it, sir. What a crowd after the concert."

Tagger smiled. "Thanks, Officer Johnson. You just gave two people an alibi if it took you that long. But it looks like we won't need them."

She nodded and looked out of breath.

Megan looked at Lisa, "Are you still planning to return to Atlanta tonight? I can check with the B&B?"

"Thanks, but we need to get back. I've already shown Tammy how to change the passwords when she reconnects their computers. We'll be gone shortly. I'm leaving this doomsday computer with you, Sheriff Tagger. Your techs still need to look at it and study this worm Susan created. She would have been a brilliant programmer. Too bad she chose a life of crime, or should I say, a life of ease?"

They all said their goodbyes, packed up what needed to be done, and left. Derek reflected everyone seemed to feel a sense of sadness beneath the relief of discovery. Sadness at knowing a man was killed and an abused young woman chose a self-destructive turn in a life that had started with such promise.

Megan walked beside Derek on the fast-emptying streets. She said in a soft voice echoing his thoughts. So sad. "Adam Cranford's story reminds me of a Bible verse."

"Which one? There are so many that apply. 'Do Not Steal,' is one that leaps to my mind."

"I was thinking of the story in Luke 12 about the man who had an abundant harvest one year. Instead of sharing or helping others, he built bigger barns to store his surplus grain. And he decided that since he had plenty of grain laid up for many years, he would take life easy and 'eat, drink and be merry.' However, God said, 'You fool! This very night your life will be demanded from you. Then who will get what you have prepared for yourself? This is how it will be with whoever stores up things for themselves but is not rich toward God.' I think that applies to Adam. He spent his life sneaking and stealing instead of spending time with his family and really enjoying life. Then just before he was ready to 'eat, drink, and be merry,' God took his life. Some stranger got what he prepared for himself."

Derek thought for a moment. "Adam missed out on a lot, didn't he? He could have had a family that respected him and grandchildren to love. He could have had friends that enjoyed his company. I have found no one that liked him or trusted him. He chose to focus on getting even with imaginary enemies and accumulating money he would never use."

He put his arm around Megan as they walked, and she leaned her head against his shoulder. She said, "A cautionary tale. Let's be smarter and spend our money as God directs."

Chapter 23:
Justice

The next morning, Derek and Megan enjoyed a leisurely breakfast in the dining room at the B&B. They had found the special large Sunday breakfast buffet a challenge but were up to it. They were discussing which local church to visit for Sunday morning services when Sheriff Tagger walked into the room.

Sheriff Tagger nodded at his sister-in-law who was refilling the buffet. She waved back and asked him if he wanted a free breakfast. He grinned and shook his head "no."

He sat down at Derek and Megan's table. "We found Sergio."

"Where?" asked Derek.

"Not good. He and his car are at the bottom of a lake in South Georgia. When a new auditor began looking into Fenwood's books a couple of days ago, it was discovered that Sergio had found major fraud and coverup by the Fenwood Corporation. Adam was blackmailing Dorothy Fenwood. Her father, Darren, was paying the money, and then writing them off as a business expense under legal costs. As Susan indicated last night, since Adam was a criminal attorney, Sergio questioned it and wanted to find out more information.

So, he visited Adam and asked his questions. Adam realized he held Darren in the palm of his hands if he said he had not been giving them business advice. But of even more importance to Sergio's investigation, the Fenbrook Corporation was defrauding the government on a massive scale. Both brothers were brought in for questioning yesterday. Brother Barry offered to cut a deal. He revealed that Darren had kidnapped Sergio at his home and then killed him after forcing him to send some emails saying he went away. Of course, Darren is denying it and claiming Barry did it. But given Susan's statements last night, it looks like Darren is the guilty party. Furthermore, Darren is an excellent shot and was in special ops. Sergio's family may consider it good news, in a way. Investigators found the body to provide closure on his disappearance for them. Also, we showed he didn't abandon them and was not a traitor."

"That's certainly a relief for them, but I'm surprised it's so quick," exclaimed Derek.

"The proof had already been found by Sergio. No one had looked for it before in his records. Also, four years of a guilty conscience and waiting to hear the other shoe drop must have weakened Brother Barry's resistance, especially if he's not a killer and knew what his brother did. So, the way I'm looking at it is Darren knew his daughter could no longer be charged, no matter what evidence Adam had. The statute of limitations had just run out. He knows Sergio is after him and facing major jail time and fines, so kills Sergio. He then kills Adam to remove him as a witness against him but also as revenge for all the years he'd paid blackmail for his daughter.

Derek nodded. He was glad to end his detective

career knowing he had helped expose a long dormant killer.

Megan said, "So Sheriff Tagger, what about Susan Weaver? Have you had a chance to talk to the D.A. yet?"

"That's not for public consumption, if you want to know for that article you're writing."

"That and just curiosity."

"Off the record, he's thinking about it. I can't say more than that. But, he does want that tape. We don't even know if she's in a country that shares extradition with the U.S. She could be beyond reach, at least for now."

Derek said, "Even if she were brought here, a jury might have sympathy for her acting on impulse in a moment of crisis. What they would have trouble overlooking is that she kept quiet for four years."

Tagger said, "Another reason the D.A. is considering it. He is talking to her attorney. They have exchanged contact information."

Megan said, "So, you not only have your cold case killer and a thief exposed, but in your town a very nice Christian family has been cleared of a dark cloud of suspicion. Farther south in Georgia, a family has found closure for a missing man presumed to be a traitor but shown to be loyal to his family, country, and his job. At least that's the way my articles will describe this story."

Tagger smiled at Megan and said, "Very true." He looked at Derek, "Are you sure you want to go to law school, Fielding? There are a lot of lawyers around, but we need good detectives."

Derek smiled. "We need good lawyers, too. I will work to be a good one. But you never know. Being married to Megan, I might help solve more mysteries in the future."

Tagger offered a suggestion, "I hear William's looking for a new law partner. Maybe you should check with him after you get out. Or, even better, apply for an internship as a student."

Derek looked thoughtful.

Megan said, "God opens the doors for us to walk through. Maybe we'll be back for a visit soon."

Sheriff Tagger said, "I hope so, but no more cold cases."

Megan nodded. She preferred an active case.

About the Author

Joan Hetzler has been a freelance writer and editor for over twenty-five years. Her creative writing experience includes plays, poems, short stories, humor, memoir, and classic mystery novels. For eight years, she produced and hosted The Writers Show, a radio program devoted to writers and their readers at a local college station. From the coastal islands of South Georgia to the mountains of Northwest Georgia, Joan captures her experiences in stories and poems that reflect the glory of God.

Follow Joan on social media and her website.

www.joanhetzler.com

Bookbub:

https://www.bookbub.com/authors/joan-hetzler-4e3c75ea-562d-4dd0-9df8-ac761b6f9561

Facebook:

https://www.facebook.com/joan.hetzler.96

Twitter is @HetzlerJoan

Amazon:

Amazon.com: Joan Hetzler: books, biography, latest update

Other books by Joan:

Pious Deception

Relative Truth

Fair Game

Milton Keynes UK
Ingram Content Group UK Ltd.
UKHW021833040923
428043UK00013B/1626